METROPOLIS MASTERY

KULSUM HUSAIN

Dedication

for Huz, who never asked for anything, and gave me
everything.

Contents

Chapter 1

Mastery of the Maze

Ah, the mornings of Mumbai—treacherous lullabies of calm before the inevitable deluge of pandemonium, lull you into a false sense of calm. The rain had arrived with its usual nonchalance, streaking windows and turning streets into mirrors, but Indranil "Indro" Sen wasn't going to let it ruin his optimism. Dressed in a crisp white shirt and spotless sneakers, armed with his protein shake, he adjusted his glasses in Betsy, his trusty hatchback, and declared, "Today, the roads will make sense."

It was the kind of hopeful mantra a man in equities research might repeat daily. Numbers, after all, had a way of revealing patterns amidst the city's seeming unpredictability. Surely, Mumbai's traffic could too—though that might have been wishful thinking.

The Western Express Highway, with its deceptive calm, soon shattered any remnants of Indro's optimism. A silver SUV loomed in his rearview mirror, its high beams flashing with the urgency of a commuter who had mistaken his morning routine for a Formula 1 qualifier. Indro sighed.

"Mumbai's Morse code: move or be moved."

He shifted slightly, letting the SUV hurtle past, only to smirk as it screeched to a halt at the next red light. "Poetic justice," he muttered, reaching for his protein shake. But as the light turned green and the inevitable chorus of honking erupted, the shaker slipped from his grasp, performed a spectacular arc, and splattered its contents across the passenger seat.

The door opened abruptly, and Tasha Deshmukh, her arrival as sudden and confident as the monsoon itself, slid into the seat. As she adjusted her seatbelt, she added with a casual smile, "By the way, I've got a patient waiting at nine at Iridia Dental, so let's avoid any creative detours, shall we?" She was dressed in a storm-gray raincoat, her faint rose scent cutting through the dampness of the car.

"Smooth," she said, surveying the spill. "Still Mumbai's most graceful driver?"

Indro grabbed a tissue and began blotting at the mess. "Do you just teleport into my car? Betsy deserves better."

"Betsy and I have an understanding," Tasha replied, fastening her seatbelt. "And I needed a ride. The rain is relentless." Indro glanced at Tasha's running shoes, now faintly muddy. "So, you've already conquered the gym this morning? What time do you wake up—during the night shift?"

Tasha settled into her seat; her smile unwavering. "Somewhere between five and 'too early for sarcasm.' A quick five-kilometre run, and the world feels manageable—until Mumbai traffic reminds me otherwise."

Indro snorted. "Ah yes, clarity. Nothing screams mental zen like voluntarily running to nowhere and then sitting in this city's daily demolition derby."

"It's called discipline, Indro. Something you might learn if you weren't busy grumbling about the state of civic virtue."

"Civic virtue," he mused, dodging a two-wheeler that swerved past Betsy. "You mean the noble art of honking at every opportunity? I should've studied that instead of econometrics."

Tasha chuckled. "And yet here you are, navigating spreadsheets all day. Isn't that like running marathons with numbers?"

"At least my spreadsheets don't honk," Indro replied, expertly avoiding a wayward auto-rickshaw.

"No, they just ruin your sleep," Tasha shot back. "Tell me, when was the last time your portfolio projections didn't give you night terrors?"

"Last week. When I didn't look at them."

Her laugh cut through the drumming rain as Indro muttered, "Mumbai: where we jog for clarity and drive for pandemonium."

At the intersection of Linking Road and SV Road, the traffic resembled a symphony of discordant horns. Signal lights had abandoned their post, leaving drivers to a Darwinian free-for-all. A kind-hearted figure in a neon jacket, armed with a whistle, stood amidst the disarray like an optimistic gladiator in an arena of hatchbacks and rickshaws.

"What's this? Mumbai's very own traffic whisperer?" Indro quipped, watching as the man orchestrated the mess with all the grace of a composer conducting a reluctant orchestra.

"He's got style," Tasha remarked. "Look at that bow—like he's accepting an award for Best in Improvised Urban Management."

The whistle blew, and the Samaritan held up a hand to halt a scooter attempting to snake its way past a sedan. "There's a man who believes in miracles," Indro muttered. "Stopping a Mumbai scooterist is like convincing rain to fall upwards."

With a theatrical flourish, the Samaritan waved the vehicles forward, his movements reminiscent of Bollywood choreography. "He's Mumbai's answer to Fred Astaire," Tasha said, laughing. "Though I doubt Fred had to dodge potholes."

As they drove past, Indro noted the gratitude in the honks trailing behind. "Perhaps Mumbai doesn't need smarter lights—just braver optimists."

Drawing closer to the Andheri flyover, the rain took on a conspiratorial note, cloaking the chaos in watery ambiguity., the rain intensified, cascading down in a curtain that blurred even the most vibrant billboards. A motorcyclist zigzagged between cars with the agility of an Olympic gymnast and the logic of a particularly indecisive squirrel.

"This city's roads are a stress test," Indro muttered, gripping the wheel tightly.

Tasha tilted her head, amused. "Stress makes life interesting. Schopenhauer said life swings between pain and boredom. Mumbai, at least, spares us boredom."

"Schopenhauer," Indro replied, "never sat in Mumbai traffic."

Ahead, a car was parked diagonally across two slots, its owner scrolling through his phone with the serenity of someone entirely oblivious to the social contract.

"Ah, Parking Percy," Tasha said, watching with detached curiosity. "Mumbai's champion of spatial entitlement."

"More like a one-man urban planning disaster," Indro muttered, steering around the obstruction.

As they waited at the next signal, a parking attendant appeared, waving his hands like a conductor of turmoil. "Sir, you must park here!" he announced with an authority reserved for emperors, pointing emphatically to a muddy, half-flooded space.

"I'm not parking," Indro replied through the half-open window. "I'm driving."

"Still, sir! Best parking spot!" the attendant declared, undeterred.

"Clearly," Tasha quipped, her laughter bubbling. "He's guarding it like it's a throne."

"Or a minefield," Indro added, shaking his head as the light turned green. Their usual route seemed promising until an orange barricade loomed into view, accompanied by a handwritten sign that read, "Road Closed. Sorry."

"'Sorry'? That's all?" Tasha exclaimed. "No detour instructions, no warning—just a heartfelt apology?"

Indro sighed, glaring at the sign as though sheer force of will might make it reconsider. "It's Mumbai's version of 'good luck.'"

The detour led them through a labyrinth of narrow lanes, each more inventive than the last. One included a vegetable vendor who had decided the road was prime real estate. "I didn't realize we were grocery shopping," Indro muttered, swerving to avoid an enthusiastic shopper waving coriander.

As they rejoined the main road, Tasha shook her head. "No maps, no warnings, just chaos. It's like playing musical chairs with a city planner."

"And we're always the ones left standing," Indro added.

They hadn't gone more than a few meters when an auto-rickshaw splashed a wave of rainwater directly onto Betsy's windshield. "It's like being baptized by chaos," Indro grumbled, switching on the wipers. The rickshaw, meanwhile, weaved dangerously close to a speeding taxi, its driver apparently unfazed by physics or mortality.

"That's Mumbai's version of synchronized swimming," Tasha said, her voice tinged with admiration. "Except the judges are fate and sheer audacity."

"You'd think overtaking came with an Olympic medal," Indro added, watching as the taxi attempted to pass the rickshaw from the left, narrowly missing a biker wobbling under a precariously stacked load of plastic chairs.

"Gold medal in creative recklessness," Tasha quipped. "And the biker gets silver for balancing act."

The traffic thickened near a particularly notorious roundabout where drivers seemed to adopt the philosophy that the shortest distance between two points was a direct diagonal, regardless of lanes or logic. A hatchback darted in front of Betsy, its driver oblivious to Indro's glare.

"Do people even know what indicators are for?" Indro said, his frustration spilling over. "Or do they think those are just festive lights?"

"Indicators are merely suggestions here," Tasha remarked, her voice light but with an edge of philosophical resignation. "Like speed limits. Or lanes. Or, you know, the general concept of laws."

As if to join the existential debate, Betsy wheezed to a halt in front of an unexpected barricade—a lone, fraying rope stretched across the intended right turn. No signs, no warnings—just a limp, unapologetic obstacle, swaying slightly in the breeze as though daring drivers to decode its cryptic message.

"A rope," Indro muttered, leaning forward. "Mumbai's latest traffic innovation. Who needs road signs when you've got household items doing the job?"

Tasha tilted her head, studying it as though she'd stumbled upon a modern art installation. "Perhaps it's symbolic. A statement on the fragility of human ambition."

"Or it's just rope," Indro countered. "Either way, it's ruined my shortcut."

Behind them, a symphony of horns erupted as irate drivers leaned out of their windows, gesturing wildly. One particularly animated man yelled something that sounded suspiciously like an offer to untie it with his teeth.

"Impressive teamwork," Tasha quipped, watching as a scooterist ducked under the rope with the kind of daring normally reserved for action films.

Indro sighed, reversed, and muttered, "Mumbai doesn't need engineers. It needs interpreters." Betsy groaned her agreement as they rejoined the chaos, leaving the rope to flutter smugly in the breeze.

The honks behind them intensified. A particularly enthusiastic auto-rickshaw driver leaned out of his vehicle to shout something unintelligible. "He's probably demanding a written explanation," Indro muttered, reversing. "Or proposing a duel."

The rope remained, indifferent to the rising chaos. "Maybe it's a metaphor," Tasha suggested. "Life's obstacles can't always be understood."

"Or it's just rope," Indro replied, swerving into a detour. "Mumbai specializes in unexplained barricades."

They drove off, leaving behind the honking symphony and a rope that seemed almost smug in its triumph. As Betsy slowed to navigate a particularly chaotic stretch, a drenched orange tabby darted across the road, pausing just long enough to glare at the honking traffic with regal disdain. Tasha's face lit up. "Nugget!" she exclaimed, her tone soft as if greeting an old friend.

"Nugget?" Indro asked, watching her rummage in her bag. "You have a pre-existing relationship with this cat?"

"I call every cat Nugget," Tasha replied, rolling down her window and extending a hand. The cat, unimpressed, flicked its tail and slinked away into the shadows. Tasha sighed wistfully. "They're all treasures, just waiting to be found."

Indro didn't respond immediately. Growing up, he'd spent countless hours rescuing strays, his childhood defined by mismatched furballs and endless bowls of milk. Watching her now, he couldn't help but smile. "You know," he said, "I think that one might've preferred Sir Nugget."

"Ah, Mumbai's infamous lunar exhibits," Indro muttered, tapping the wheel. "If NASA ever runs out of craters, they can borrow this one. I'd call it 'The Grand Potholian.'"

Before Tasha could retort, a figure emerged at the edge of the commotion, battling a rebellious umbrella that flapped like an overzealous flag of surrender. Indro squinted. "Wait— is that Professor Menon? What's he doing here? Conducting a study on the velocity of despair?"

Tasha smirked. "More likely trying to hitchhike out of this mess. The pothole probably swallowed his sense of direction first."

As they inched closer, Menon spotted them and waved enthusiastically, umbrella now resembling a tragic prop from a forgotten play. Indro sighed, pulling over. "Brace yourself for the storm of wisdom."

Menon clambered in, bringing with him a tidal wave of rainwater and unshaken cheer. "Indranil! The man who once argued that regression analysis was an art form. And who is this enchanting co-pilot?"

Tasha offered a polite smile. "Tasha."

Menon raised an eyebrow, his expression both intrigued and mischievous. "Ah, a Tasha. A name that suggests elegance, mischief, and the ability to keep you in line."

Indro cleared his throat, gripping the wheel tighter. "She's a friend."

"Friend," Menon echoed, his tone rich with theatrical suspicion. "I see. A very well-chosen friend."

Tasha's laugh rang out, light and unaffected, as Indro shot Menon a glare so pointed it could have pierced the rain.

The moment was interrupted by a motorcyclist attempting to skirt the pothole with all the agility of a circus acrobat. His flip-flop, less agile, abandoned him mid-leap, sailing into the air like a startled pigeon. The ensuing traffic honks reached a crescendo as the rider hopped off to retrieve it, managing to block two lanes in the process.

"Ah, another metaphor," Menon said, unperturbed. "Life is full of obstacles. Some, like this pothole, are deep and unyielding. Others, like that flip-flop, are entirely self-inflicted."

"Meanwhile," Indro muttered, "we're all stuck because a sandal has more airtime than Mumbai's planning commission."

The motorcyclist finally retrieved his errant footwear and sped off, leaving the pothole undefeated. Menon watched it recede in the rearview mirror. "A triumph of neglect. Perhaps we should apply for UNESCO heritage status."

"Or turn it into a pop-up café," Tasha quipped, her laughter carrying them forward as Betsy rejoined the fray.

As they approached the Bandra-Worli Sea Link, the rain intensified, turning the bridge into a waterlogged runway. Cars slowed to a crawl, hazard lights blinking in chaotic unison.

"Why is it," Indro began, his voice tinged with exasperation, "that hazard lights are a universal distress signal everywhere else, but here they're the equivalent of 'I feel like being invisible today'?"

"Perhaps they think the rain justifies existential confusion," Tasha replied. "Nothing says 'I'm having a crisis' quite like flashing hazard lights in a moving car."

Menon chimed in from the back. "It's like they've decided that being indecisive is a form of enlightenment. 'Am I turning? Am I stopping? Who knows? Not even me!'"

Tasha laughed lightly. "I think they're just trying to make a statement. 'Look at me—I'm a paradox on wheels.'"

Indro shook his head. "Or worse—they believe the hazard lights are a magical cloak of invincibility. 'If I flash these, I can stop wherever I want, no consequences.'"

The car ahead, its hazard lights blinking in frantic staccato, came to an abrupt halt in the middle of the road, causing a symphony of honks to erupt behind it. Indro groaned. "Case in point."

"Maybe they're auditioning for a disco revival," Tasha suggested, her tone dry. "Hazard lights as choreography."

"Or," Menon added, his voice laced with mock seriousness, "a modern art installation. 'Chaos: A Performance Piece.'"

Indro steered Betsy around the offending vehicle, muttering under his breath. "It's like driving through a carnival where every ride is broken."

By the toll plaza, the roads unraveled into a symphony of honking and halts, each vehicle an impatient note in the score of urban life., the scene ahead unfolded like a tragic comedy. A car in the Fastag lane came to a sudden stop, its driver frantically waving cash at the attendant. Indro groaned. "Why is it always the Fastag lane? It's supposed to be fast!"

"Maybe they're nostalgic for the old ways," Tasha suggested, her voice laced with humor. "Cash has a certain charm, don't you think?"

"Charm?" Indro scoffed. "It's the vehicular equivalent of using dial-up internet in a fiber-optic world."

The car ahead finally moved, leaving a trail of disgruntled honks behind. Indro maneuvered Betsy through the toll plaza, only to have a motorcyclist cut across three lanes in front of him, narrowly avoiding a collision.

"Do they think they're starring in a Bollywood action sequence?" Indro muttered, gripping the wheel tighter.

"Or perhaps they've mistaken the toll plaza for a racing circuit," Menon chimed in. "A place where lanes are mere suggestions and speed limits are optional."

The Sea Link promised smooth sailing, but the promise was short-lived. Just as Betsy began to pick up speed, the dreaded wail of sirens echoed behind them. Traffic screeched to a halt as black SUVs barrelled past, accompanied by flashing lights and an air of undeserved self-importance.

"VIP movement," Indro muttered, gripping the wheel. "The great equalizer. Even potholes bow to them."

Tasha tilted her head. "Do they time this chaos, or is it purely instinctual disruption?"

"Instinct," Indro said. "They've trained their drivers in Advanced Inconvenience Theory."

The cavalcade sped past, leaving behind a trail of grumbling commuters. A fruit seller, caught mid-negotiation, sighed dramatically before resuming his pitch. "Even bananas must wait," Tasha quipped.

As the road reopened, Indro muttered, "They'll get stuck in their own jam soon enough. Traffic karma is real."

As they approached Nariman Point, the rain lightened, and the chaos seemed to ebb slightly. A young girl selling flowers darted between cars, her agility a testament to survival skills honed in the urban jungle. She leaned toward Betsy's window, offering a lotus.

"Didi, take a piece of the Brahman," she said, her tone both reverent and playful.

Tasha took the flower with a smile. "What's your name?"

"Meena," the girl replied, her eyes sparkling with mischief. "And I'm no philosopher, just a flower seller."

Menon nodded thoughtfully. "Sometimes, wisdom comes from the simplest sources."

"Like the lotus," Tasha added, twirling it in her fingers. "A reminder that beauty emerges even in muddy waters."

Meena grinned. "My grandfather used to say the same. He believed the lotus is like the soul—untouched by the dirt around it."

"Ah, non-duality," Menon said, his voice carrying a touch of reverence. "Where there is no separation between the soul and the world. Everything is interconnected."

Indro snorted softly. "Try explaining that to the guy who just cut me off on the Sea Link. I'm sure he'd feel very 'connected.'"

Tasha laughed. "Well, Schopenhauer might agree with Meena's grandfather. He believed in the oneness of all existence, didn't he?"

"Yes," Menon replied. "But Schopenhauer would also have grumbled about the honking. He had no patience for unnecessary noise."

"Then he wouldn't last five minutes in Mumbai," Indro said. "Here, honking is the city's second language."

At another intersection, they encountered a peculiar scene: a man proudly holding up a weathered driving license, arguing with a policeman. "This license," the man proclaimed, "has been in my family for three generations! It's practically an antique!"

Tasha chuckled. "License as heirloom. What's next, family parking spots?"

Menon, ever the philosopher, mused, "It does explain some of the driving. Skills passed down as generously as the license itself."

As they navigated another stretch of chaotic traffic, a scooter zipped past carrying an entire family—father, mother, two children, and what appeared to be a caged parrot. "And here's the grand finale," Indro said dryly. "The great Mumbai balancing act."

By the time they reached their destination, the streets glistened under the pale streetlights. Tasha stepped out first, turning back with her signature laugh. "Master the maze, Indro. Don't let it master you."

"Easier said than done," Indro muttered, but he couldn't help smiling as Betsy carried him and Menon back into the city's chaotic embrace.

Chapter 2

Mastery With the Mavericks

Indro's legs were staging what he could only describe as a deeply personal protest. Each step through the bustling corridors of Chhatrapati Shivaji Maharaj International Airport was an exercise in perseverance, accompanied by noises that could only be compared to the creaking of an antique armchair. Tasha, meanwhile, moved with the effortless grace of a prima ballerina moonlighting as a motivational speaker, her strides unbothered by the chaos around her.

"It's that Pavel Tuh-suh-tou-line routine," Indro muttered, dragging his carry-on bag with all the enthusiasm of a man reluctantly fulfilling his civic duty.

"Tsat-sou-leen," Tasha corrected, her tone light, as though she were discussing the merits of a particularly good pastry. "And your legs will thank me when you can climb stairs without resembling a giraffe on roller skates."

"My legs," Indro replied, adjusting the strap on his bag, "are drafting their memoirs. The title? Life and Times of Two Overworked Appendages. Spoiler: there's no happy ending."

Tasha chuckled, patting his shoulder with mock sympathy. "Don't worry; pain builds character. You'll thank me when you discover the joys of endorphins."

"Character?" Indro shot back, his expression sour. "I'm already brimming with it. What I need is a stretcher and a well-funded retirement plan for my knees."

"Fitness camaraderie," Tasha said breezily, "is about shared struggle. You'd know that if you actually committed to it instead of grumbling your way out after every session."

Indro gave her a look that could have wilted flowers. "Shared struggle? That sounds suspiciously like propaganda. I prefer team sports, where at least there are teammates to take the blame when things go wrong."

Tasha slowed her pace slightly, her gaze flicking toward him with an almost imperceptible softness. "Teammates," she repeated. "You always mention them. Did you play any sports growing up?"

Indro hesitated, a rare flicker of vulnerability crossing his face. "Not really. Never had the chance, I guess. Too much schoolwork, not enough time." He gave a wry smile. "And no one to push me into it, either."

She didn't press further, though her tone shifted, gentler now. "Well, dumbbells can be teammates too," she said lightly.

"They're reliable. They don't hog the ball or skip practice. And they're always there to help you improve."

"That's because they're inanimate objects," Indro muttered, sidestepping a toddler dragging a backpack that appeared to contain a small planet. "You can't have camaraderie with something that doesn't have a pulse."

"Ah," Tasha said, her grin widening as they approached the check-in counters. "So, your real problem isn't exercise. It's the lack of an audience for your suffering."

Indro opened his mouth to retort but was interrupted by a trolley loaded with precariously stacked suitcases hurtling past like a slow-moving avalanche. He turned back to her, his expression resigned. "If you're going to push this gym camaraderie agenda, you'd better promise there won't be another Pavel routine waiting for me."

"No promises," she replied, her laugh ringing out as they joined the chaos of the airport.

Indro's protein shaker was more than a mere container of suspiciously green liquid—it was his self-prescribed fortress against the germ apocalypse he was certain awaited him on the flight. He shook it tentatively, each rattle suggesting the contents were less a health drink and more an act of rebellion against culinary decency.

"I'll drink this before the flight," he announced, his tone lofty, "to fortify my immune system. You know how it is. Planes are just airborne petri dishes for people who don't understand that coughing into their elbows is a global courtesy."

Tasha, gliding beside him with the effortless elegance of someone who had never been burdened by existential dread in liquid form, raised an eyebrow. "Fortification? That's an ambitious word for what looks like liquid grass clippings."

"It's not grass clippings," Indro snapped, giving the shaker another cautious rattle. "It's... science. Protein, antioxidants, spinach—"

"Ah, spinach," Tasha interrupted, her amusement barely concealed. "The ingredient that says, 'I care about health, but not about flavor.'"

Indro adjusted his bag and shook the container more vigorously, as though trying to assert dominance over its unruly contents. "You'll see. While the entire plane is symphonically hacking into the recycled air, I'll be the picture of vitality."

"You'll also be the only one glowing green from the inside out," Tasha quipped. "Trouble in hydration paradise?"

"It's fine," Indro said, tightening the lid with the care of a man handling a rare artifact. "Perfectly under control."

"Perfectly," Tasha echoed, her grin widening. "You look like you're taming a wild animal. Did you even measure the ingredients, or is this another one of your culinary experiments?"

Indro ignored her, though his grip on the shaker suggested her jab had landed. "Gym people overcomplicate everything," he muttered. "Just because you put spinach in something doesn't mean it's healthy—or edible."

"Spinach," Tasha mused, nodding thoughtfully. "The vegetable that refuses to be liked. Even your drink doesn't want to associate with it."

"I'll have you know," Indro replied, shaking the container with renewed vigor, "that this is a scientifically balanced post-workout blend. Protein, antioxidants, and enough good bacteria to make even a flight attendant proud."

"Balanced?" Tasha tilted her head. "Like your gym bag, which I'm pretty sure contains everything except a commitment to fitness?"

Indro shot her a look. "At least my gym bag doesn't laugh at me."

"That's because it doesn't have a pulse," Tasha said, clearly enjoying herself. "Unlike dumbbells, which you treat like they weigh ten times more than they actually do."

Indro opened his mouth to retort but was interrupted by a brisk traveler barreling past them with a hurried "Excuse me!" The traveler didn't wait for a response, disappearing into the crowd like a particularly demanding ghost.

"Do you think anyone ever actually means 'excuse me'?" Tasha asked. "It's just a demand dressed up as a question."

Indro smirked, his grip on the shaker loosening. "The only way to test that theory is to say 'no.' Spoiler alert: it doesn't end well."

Tasha laughed lightly, shaking her head. "People aren't trying to be rude. They're just in their own little worlds."

He glanced at her, his expression softening. For all her sharp wit, Tasha's ability to forgive the quirks of human nature never ceased to amaze him. "You're too patient, you know that?"

"Maybe," she said, her grin returning. "But if I weren't, I wouldn't be standing here watching you shake that thing like it owes you money."

"Patience," Indro muttered, giving the shaker one last determined rattle. "That's the only thing this drink and I have in common."

The protein shaker had other plans. With one final, defiant shake, the lid surrendered to the pressure, sending the contents into an airborne pirouette before splattering back to earth in an arc of spectacular chaos.

Tasha, blessed with the reflexes of someone well-practiced in avoiding gym disasters, stepped back just in time to avoid the splash zone. Her wide-eyed gaze took in the scene before her—Indro, frozen in horror, now liberally coated in what could generously be described as "health sludge."

"Well," Tasha began, her voice trembling with barely suppressed laughter. "Perfectly under control, was it?"

Indro stared at her, then down at the spreading puddle at his feet. "Refreshing," he said finally, with the resigned tone of a man who had learned to pick his battles.

Tasha's composure cracked, and she burst out laughing, her mirth drawing the attention of several passersby, including a toddler who pointed at the mess with the gleeful curiosity of a child discovering gravity for the first time. "I should have recorded that," she managed between giggles. "You'd go viral on YouTube. Man vs. Shaker: A Cautionary Tale."

Indro, attempting to salvage what little dignity he had left, rummaged through his bag and produced a napkin that could charitably be described as undersized for the job. "Fitness influencers on YouTube," he muttered, dabbing at his shirt, "are just salespeople for chaos. They make this look easy, but it's all lies."

Tasha wiped a tear from the corner of her eye, shaking her head. "Don't be so dramatic. You're just living the authentic fitness experience."

"Authentic?" Indro shot back, his voice dripping with sarcasm. "Authentically humiliating, maybe. This shake is the only thing getting a workout today."

He crouched to assess the spill, which had now become a minor attraction in the airport's bustling corridor. Nearby, a man stepped gingerly around the puddle, casting Indro a look that seemed equal parts sympathy and amusement. "You'd think," Indro muttered, "that a place with this many footfalls would have cleaning wipes dispensers. It's basic logistics."

Tasha, still chuckling, tilted her head thoughtfully. "I think Narita Airport in Tokyo has those. You spill, you clean. Simple, efficient, polite."

"Of course it does," Indro said, exhaling in frustration. "Leave it to Japan to think of the obvious while we're stuck trying to mop up chaos with a napkin and a prayer."

A janitor finally appeared, armed with a mop and the expression of someone who had seen far worse. Indro straightened, offering an apologetic nod. "I promise this was an accident. And," he added, casting a sidelong glance at Tasha, "not entirely my fault."

"Not entirely?" Tasha raised an eyebrow, her grin threatening to break free again. "You were the one shaking it like it was auditioning for a dance show."

Indro sighed and stuffed the now-empty shaker back into his bag. "You laugh, but I was only trying to fortify myself for the plane. At least the germs won't have a fighting chance."

"Not against the sludge, no," Tasha agreed, her laughter bubbling over once more as they resumed their journey through the terminal.

The check-in counter loomed ahead, a sprawling tapestry of human behavior at its most theatrical. It was less a line and more a highly adaptable ecosystem, constantly morphing, thriving in a way that defied both logic and basic human decency.

Families huddled in tense negotiations over baggage weights, each kilogram a battleground for familial pride and possibly the inheritance of a favorite pressure cooker. An elderly man clutched a sheaf of tickets as though he were a priest deciphering ancient scrolls, while a child zigzagged through the chaos wielding a sticky lollipop that gleamed like a medieval mace, its orbit of sugar leaving casualties in the form of stained trousers and frazzled tempers.

Indro sighed deeply. "Why can't we be like Singapore? Orderly, efficient, zen. Here, queues are less a process and more a Darwinian experiment."

Tasha, observing the scene with the air of a sociologist studying a particularly resilient species, said, "Mumbai's queues are alive. They breathe. They adapt. They consume."

"Like amoebas with roller bags," Indro muttered, stepping aside just in time to avoid a woman whose suitcase erupted like a colorful piñata, spilling scarves that seemed to multiply as they hit the floor.

Ahead of them, a man wrestled with a trolley so overstuffed it appeared he was relocating an entire village. "Why do people pack like they're moving planets?" Tasha mused, her eyes gleaming with a mixture of amusement and bewilderment.

"Family heirlooms," Indro replied, nodding sagely. "And guilt-induced gifts. Nothing says, 'Sorry I missed your birthday,' like three kilos of mithai and a pressure cooker."

Right on cue, the inevitable happened. The trolley toppled in slow motion, scattering bags, shoes, and the aforementioned pressure cooker across the floor in a scene that could only be described as tragically inevitable. The amoeba-like travelers barely paused, shifting fluidly around the debris as though it were part of their natural habitat.

Tasha raised an eyebrow. "Adaptation at its finest."

"Survival of the lightest," Indro added, gesturing to a woman who glided past with only a slim handbag, her disdain for checked luggage evident in her confident stride.

As they inched forward, a man at the counter ahead began a spirited debate with the clerk over his overweight bag, producing what appeared to be a fruitcake as his final attempt at appeasement.

"What's in that bag?" Tasha whispered to Indro. "Gold bricks?"

"Close," Indro replied, deadpan. "Emotional baggage."

Tasha chuckled, then gestured toward a nearby display screen looping a video of impeccably packed luggage sets being loaded into a pristine cargo hold. "You know, it's this kind of visual propaganda that ruins people. These YouTube videos make packing look effortless. They never show you the part where someone has to sit on the suitcase to zip it shut."

Indro smirked. "That's the problem with video content. It makes everything look polished, like life is just one long montage set to peppy music. No spilled scarves, no toppling trolleys."

"True," Tasha said. "But text-based platforms, like Reddit, at least show the mess. You get threads like, 'What's the most ridiculous thing you've seen at an airport?' And the comments are pure gold."

Indro nodded thoughtfully. "Reading lets you imagine the chaos. Watching it sanitizes the mess. You can almost believe it's manageable—until you're here, dodging flying fruitcakes and collapsing trolleys."

Tasha's gaze softened. "You sound nostalgic. Did your family have strict packing protocols?"

"Strict?" Indro said, his expression warming. "Packing with my mother and aunts was a military operation. Every inch of space accounted for, every item vetted for necessity. Chaos was unacceptable." He hesitated, then added, "I guess it's why I find this... unsettling."

Tasha smiled. "You're drawn to order. I like that about you. But you know, there's a charm in the mess, too. It's human."

Indro glanced at her, surprised by the observation, but said nothing. Ahead, the man with the fruitcake finally conceded defeat, handing over the offending item to the clerk like a martyr relinquishing his worldly possessions.

"Shall we?" Tasha asked, gesturing forward with a grin. At security, Indro steeled himself for the symphony of beeps, the cacophony of trays clattering, and the grumbling chorus of travelers fumbling with shoes and belts. It was a concert he had attended far too often, but the performers always managed to deliver a unique medley of exasperation. Ahead of them, a man waved his arms with the desperation of someone attempting to flag down a plane mid-flight.

"It's for my grandmother!" he pleaded, holding up a jar of honey as though it were the Holy Grail. "She's 92, and she swears by it!"

"It exceeds 100 ml, sir," the officer replied, his tone flat but with the faintest hint of practiced patience. He confiscated the jar with the precision of a surgeon and the finality of a judge.

"Ah," Tasha murmured, leaning toward Indro. "The sentimental smugglers. They never learn."

"It's the emotional math," Indro replied. "They think 'for my grandmother' cancels out international aviation laws. Someone should tell them it's not an equation."

The man continued to protest, his impassioned argument now attracting the attention of onlookers. Tasha smiled faintly but said nothing, her gaze momentarily distant.

"My mother always said," she began quietly, "that the only things worth carrying are stories and songs. She never had much patience for clutter."

Indro glanced at her, noting the slight shift in her tone. "Sounds like she was practical."

"She was," Tasha replied, her voice soft. "Practical, disciplined, and… impossible to impress."

Indro's brow furrowed, but he let the comment hang in the air, knowing better than to prod further. Instead, he gestured toward the scene ahead, where the jar of honey was now being dropped unceremoniously into a bin labeled Prohibited Items.

"This is definitely one for Reddit," Indro said, his tone light. "I can already see the thread: 'r/travelfails—man tries to smuggle honey, ends up creating airport drama.'"

Tasha laughed, her momentary introspection dissolving. "The comments would be the best part. 'Was the honey worth the humiliation?'"

"'He'll never look at bees the same way again,'" Indro added, a smirk tugging at his lips.

They passed through security without further incident, emerging into the baggage area where chaos continued its reign. Indro's attention was immediately drawn to a black-and-white cat sprawled near the luggage carousel, its tail flicking lazily as if to suggest it was entirely unimpressed by humanity's struggles.

"You've got to be kidding me," Indro said, his voice a blend of disbelief and resignation.

"Nugget!" Tasha exclaimed, crouching instantly.

"That's not Nugget," Indro protested. "That's just... an airport cat."

"All cats are Nugget," Tasha replied firmly, extending her hand with the slow, practiced grace of someone fluent in feline diplomacy.

The cat regarded her with the cautious curiosity of a monarch evaluating a new subject. After a moment, it sniffed her fingers and emitted a soft, gravelly meow before rubbing against her leg with the kind of deliberate affection that made humans feel chosen.

"Did you know," Tasha said, scratching behind its ears, "that cats only meow for humans? It's their way of communicating with us."

"Great," Indro muttered, his tone perfectly level. "Bilingual and entitled—just the sort of attitude that thrives around here."

He said nothing about the afternoons spent with his aunts rescuing caged birds, gently coaxing the frightened creatures to take their first hesitant steps into freedom. Those moments had taught him the quiet joy of care, the kind that didn't require recognition or fanfare. But this was a memory he chose to keep to himself, finding a quiet comfort in the unspoken understanding that seemed to exist between him and Tasha—a shared compassion that didn't need to be spelled out.

Instead, he added dryly, "Although, to be fair, this one seems far better at crowd management than most of the staff here."

Tasha's laughter came easily, and in the warmth of that sound, Indro felt the moment settle comfortably between them—light, unspoken, and quietly memorable.

The cat purred, its trust seemingly complete, before sauntering off toward the baggage carts. Just as it disappeared, a commotion broke out nearby—a man in an ill-fitting suit was gesticulating wildly at a ground staff member, his voice climbing into a register usually reserved for amateur opera. The jostling and raised voices startled the cat, sending it darting away into the shadows.

Tasha sighed, brushing her hands on her jumpsuit. "That," she said with a wistful smile, "is why airports aren't all bad. There's always a Nugget somewhere."

"Until someone tries to claim it as excess baggage," Indro quipped.

Tasha laughed, her eyes still scanning the spot where the cat had vanished. "Or posts it on Reddit: 'Airport Cat: A Day in the Life.'"

Indro shook his head, but he couldn't help the grin spreading across his face. "Well, Nugget, wherever you are, good luck surviving this circus."

The boarding gate was less a functional part of the airport and more a social experiment in organized chaos. Despite clear announcements about boarding zones, passengers surged forward as though the plane were Noah's last ark, with limited room and a divine deadline. The result was a human traffic jam, with people standing so close that their boarding passes might as well have been communal property.

Indro clutched his boarding pass like a talisman, muttering, "Every time. It's like watching a stampede, but less organized."

"Stampedes," Tasha replied, her tone dry, "at least have survival instincts. This is just herd mentality."

The queue—or what could generously be called a queue—shuffled forward. A toddler in light-up sneakers took it upon himself to explore the area, his zigzagging path causing enough disruption to qualify as an Olympic event. Indro stepped aside just in time to avoid a collision, while the child's parent offered a half-hearted "Sorry," before returning to their phone.

"Classic boarding gate behavior," Indro said. "Zero situational awareness. I'm surprised no one's holding a conference call from here."

"Give it a minute," Tasha replied. "There's still time for someone to FaceTime their entire extended family."

Nearby, a man was loudly declaring his allegiance to Zone 2, despite holding a Zone 4 boarding pass. "But it's all the same plane!" he exclaimed, waving the pass like a revolutionary banner.

"That's the problem with proximity," Tasha mused. "People assume it gives them priority."

Indro raised an eyebrow. "Is that philosophy, or did you just make that up?"

"Both," she said, stepping forward as their zone was called.

Optimistically past the boarding gate, the line paused yet again, this time plunging them into the purgatory of the walkway leading to the plane. The air was thick, stagnant, and filled with the awkward shuffling of impatient feet.

Indro scanned his surroundings, taking in the cramped, fluorescent-lit corridor and the haphazard arrangement of people trying not to make eye contact with one another. "You know," he said, adjusting his carry-on, "this walkway feels like the waiting room for judgment day. Only hotter."

Tasha smirked. "Or a sociological experiment. Put enough people in a confined space with no clear end in sight, and you can measure the breakdown of civility."

"Civility broke down at the check-in counter," Indro muttered. "This is the fallout."

A woman ahead of them sighed audibly, clutching her bag to her chest like a life raft. Nearby, a nervous man was repeatedly checking his boarding pass, his fingers twitching as though the act of looking at it would speed up the process.

"People hate uncertainty," Tasha said, observing the scene like a researcher in her natural habitat. "This is the perfect storm: confined spaces, ambiguous timelines, and no distractions."

Indro raised an eyebrow. "No distractions? You mean no Wi-Fi. If there was free Wi-Fi, everyone here would be blissfully scrolling instead of vibrating with anxiety."

Tasha tilted her head thoughtfully. "Actually, that's one of the things the ISRO scientist was talking about earlier—how tech can alleviate stress in situations like this. Imagine AI systems that could predict crowd behavior and suggest better ways to manage flow. Or even apps that give you real-time boarding updates to prevent this bottleneck."

At that moment, the line lurched forward, and a middle-aged woman with a slim leather briefcase turned to Tasha with a polite smile. "Are you traveling for work?"

"Yes," Tasha replied, grateful for the distraction. "And you?"

"I'm with ISRO," the woman said, adjusting her scarf. "Satellite communications."

Tasha's eyes lit up. "That's fascinating. What kind of projects do you work on?"

The woman explained her role in managing multilingual collaborations for satellite launches, punctuating her anecdotes with dry humor about the challenges of coordinating with engineers across continents.

"You speak five languages?" Tasha asked, impressed.

"It helps," the woman replied modestly. "Especially when trying to explain why something exploded to someone in their native tongue."

Tasha laughed, but her tone softened. "My mother always said language is a bridge. She wanted me to learn more, but I never quite had her discipline."

Indro, listening from the sidelines, was struck by the personal note. He rarely saw Tasha so reflective, and he wondered if the ISRO scientist reminded her of her mother's relentless drive for excellence.

The woman shifted to discussing AI's role in satellite data processing and its potential applications in medicine. "AI is transforming diagnostics," she said. "Imagine a world where every hospital, no matter how remote, has access to the same advanced tools."

"That's incredible," Tasha said, her voice tinged with awe. "But isn't there a risk of over-reliance?"

The scientist nodded. "Absolutely. The human element is irreplaceable, especially in critical decisions. Machines can assist, but they can't replace intuition and empathy."

Indro couldn't resist. "So, what you're saying is AI might help hospitals, but it won't make this walkway any faster?"

The scientist chuckled. "Sadly, no. But maybe one day it'll optimize boarding zones so we're not all packed like sardines here."

As they finally began boarding, Tasha turned to Indro, her eyes thoughtful. "I need to look into that. Language AI, diagnostics—it's all connected. My mother would have loved it."

Indro smiled, his usual sarcasm taking a backseat. "I'm sure she would. And you'd explain it better than any YouTube video ever could."

As they navigated the aisle toward their seats, Indro found himself in the midst of what could only be described as an airborne bazaar. Overhead bins creaked under the strain of passengers' ambitious packing, and every few steps, someone paused abruptly to fiddle with a bag, causing a chain reaction of collisions that rippled through the line like dominos in designer luggage.

Indro had just wedged his carry-on into an overhead bin that looked one zip away from structural collapse when a bright, enthusiastic voice rang out, piercing through the din.

"Indro? Is that you?"

The tone alone was enough to make him freeze mid-motion, his expression shifting into the neutral politeness of a man caught between fight and flight. "Meera," he said, turning slowly, his voice as cautious as a man addressing a suspiciously friendly tiger.

She swept toward him, a neon-pink vision of nostalgia and unchecked enthusiasm, her carry-on rattling like a suitcase full of tambourines. It was plastered with so many stickers it could have been a geography teacher's visual aid. "I can't believe it! You haven't changed a bit!"

"Neither have you," Indro replied, glancing at Tasha, who was watching the interaction with a look that suggested she was both highly entertained and mentally drafting a sitcom pitch.

"Are you two... together?" Meera asked, her tone brimming with curiosity and just a pinch of speculative hope.

"Traveling together," Tasha clarified, her smile as sharp and deliberate as a scalpel. "Where are you headed?"

"Goa!" Meera declared with the zeal of a motivational speaker. "Yoga retreat. Cleansing the soul, realigning the chakras."

Indro cleared his throat, his discomfort evident. "Sounds... enlightening."

Meera leaned conspiratorially toward Tasha. "You should come sometime. Indro could really use some chakra work. Don't you think?"

"Oh, Indro's chakras," Tasha replied, her tone velvet smooth, "are a full-time project."

Meera laughed, oblivious to the undertone, and bustled off, narrowly missing another passenger with her swinging carry-on. Indro slumped into his seat, shaking his head as Tasha slid into hers.

"Blast from the past?" Tasha inquired, her tone brimming with amusement.

"Blast is the right word," Indro muttered, tugging his seatbelt into place. "I feel like I've just been ambushed by an overly chatty tourist brochure."

Before Tasha could respond, a passenger a few rows ahead began a spirited debate with a flight attendant about whether his bag could stay in the aisle "just until takeoff."

"This is why overhead bins are always full," Indro whispered. "People think they've reserved parking spots for their luggage."

The attendant, armed with a professional smile that could have withstood a typhoon, calmly redirected him. "Sir, we need to keep the aisle clear. Please store your bag overhead."

"Where?" the man replied, gesturing dramatically at the packed bins. "I'd need a forklift to get it up there."

Meanwhile, a woman across the aisle waved frantically at another attendant. "Excuse me! Can I get a glass of water? And maybe some peanuts? Oh, and is it possible to change my seat?"

Tasha leaned toward Indro. "And they say patience is a virtue."

"Not on planes," Indro replied. "Here, it's more of an urban legend."

As the plane finally began to taxi, Meera popped up again, waving cheerfully. "Remember, Indro! Goa! Chakras! Don't forget!"

Indro gave her a weak wave, leaning back into his seat with a resigned sigh. "If I hear the word 'chakra' one more time, I'm switching to the window seat. Alone."

Tasha laughed as the engines roared and the plane lifted off. "Careful, Indro. Yoga retreats could be your destiny."

"Not unless they start serving overhead bin etiquette lessons," Indro muttered, adjusting his mismatched socks. "Now that would be enlightening."

Chapter 3

Mastery of Mocha

The Arabian Sea glimmered in shades of molten gold as the sun bowed graciously toward the horizon. Gadda Da Vida, a seaside café at Novotel Juhu, was in its prime hour. The jazz playlist, warm lighting, and the faint murmur of waves conspired to create an illusion of tranquility—a façade that was bound to crack.

Indro arrived, clutching his nearly empty protein shaker and battered notebook. He picked a table at the deck's edge, where the breeze felt like a conspiratorial nudge, encouraging him to believe, however fleetingly, that peace was possible.

He opened his notebook, intending to finish calculations for a report due the next morning. But Indro's aspirations were rarely aligned with Mumbai's chaos. The first fissure in the café's carefully curated tranquility appeared in the form of a man in a grey polo shirt stationed at the communal table. His phone was on speaker, naturally, because nothing enhances a private conversation quite like a public audience. His voice rose and fell with the dramatic flair of an operatic tenor—except his aria concerned overdue invoices and a possibly fabricated canine appetite.

"I don't care if the supplier's dog ate the invoices, Ramesh! Fix it, or find a new career!" he thundered, his hand slicing the air like a conductor leading an orchestra of doom.

Indro, hunched over his notebook filled with precise calculations for his report, paused mid-equation. "Dogs in Mumbai," he murmured under his breath, "are evolving faster than we think. Next, they'll be filing tax returns."

At the counter, a toddler clutched a tablet broadcasting an animated squirrel heist at full volume. The tinny, high-pitched squeals of the cartoon squirrels collided violently with the café's saxophone-heavy jazz playlist, creating a soundscape that could only be described as avant-garde cacophony.

Indro's pencil hovered over the page as he winced at a particularly loud metallic screech. Patrons were shifting uncomfortably in their seats, dragging chairs across the floor with the enthusiasm of a demolition crew discovering an ancient ruin.

"If chair-dragging were an Olympic sport," Indro muttered, "Mumbai would sweep the podium. Gold, silver, and bronze."

Just then, Tasha appeared, espresso in hand, her linen shirt catching the breeze as if choreographed. She slid gracefully into the seat opposite him and surveyed the scene with an arched eyebrow. "What's wrong? Don't like free jazz?"

Indro gestured toward the man in grey. "That guy just fired a dog. And over there—" he nodded at the toddler— "those squirrels are organizing a coup."

Tasha glanced over, her lips twitching in amusement. "Ah, Mumbai cafés. A haven for multi-taskers. Meetings, cartoons, and chair symphonies all rolled into one."

Indro set his pencil down and leaned back, his notebook temporarily abandoned. "I'm starting to think communal tables were invented by someone who hated silence. And chairs—why must they be dragged with such… conviction?"

"Maybe we should suggest soundproof seating," Tasha offered, sipping her espresso thoughtfully. "Or invent a noise-dampening café slipper for chairs."

Indro considered this. "That, or I'm buying noise-cancelling headphones and retiring from humanity."

Another metallic screech interrupted their musings, followed by the toddler's triumphant giggle as the squirrels onscreen completed their heist. Meanwhile, the man in grey launched into a new tirade, his voice rising above the chaos like a battle cry.

The Arabian Sea shimmered serenely in the background, blissfully detached from the discord, reminding Indro that peace, much like his calculations, was fleeting.

At the counter, a middle-aged woman in a sequined jacket debated the barista with the intensity of a litigator at the Hague. "One shot or two? No, wait—what's the difference between oat milk and almond milk? Oh, and is the mocha gluten-free?"

The line behind her began shifting with the unease of an audience unsure whether they were witnessing an avant-garde play or a hostage negotiation. Indro, clutching his nearly empty shaker, sighed. "I didn't realize coffee orders came with footnotes."

"It's not an order," Tasha replied, her tone laced with amusement. "It's a one-woman audition for 'Café Sophisticate of the Year.'"

When the barista finally handed over her drink, the woman inspected it with the precision of a jeweler evaluating a questionable gemstone. "Could you add a little less foam? And, oh dear, is this sustainably sourced?"

Behind her, a younger man in aviators executed a stealthy maneuver, sliding into the front of the line under the pretense of examining the menu board. A customer objected loudly, and a heated debate ensued, escalating with the speed and choreography of a Bollywood flash mob.

"Ah, the queue jumpers," Indro remarked dryly. "Mumbai's apex predators. No natural enemies, plenty of prey."

Tasha smirked. "Do you think we should warn him that baristas have long memories?"

"Let's leave him to discover it," Indro replied. "A barista scorned doesn't brew their best work."

As if on cue, the barista handed the young man his coffee with a smile so forced it could have been framed as modern art. The man took a sip, paused, and frowned, but before he could voice a complaint, the barista had turned to the next customer with the efficiency of a battlefield medic.

Indro leaned toward Tasha. "That's the closest thing to poetic justice this place will ever see."

He stared at his protein shaker with the sort of resigned frustration usually reserved for malfunctioning ticket machines. The shaker, untouched by any vigorous shaking, sat innocently on the table, its contents pooled at the bottom like a metaphor for unfulfilled potential.

"Just one sip," he muttered, tilting the shaker ever so slightly toward his mouth. It was a delicate operation, a balancing act between hydration and disaster.

Disaster won.

The dregs, dense and unyielding, spilled in an ungainly arc, landing with a splatter across the table. The pattern resembled the sort of abstract art that gallery curators describe as "provocative," though the only thing provoked here was Indro's temper.

Tasha, already seated across from him, hummed Auld Lang Syne under her breath, her rhythm unbroken by the unfolding chaos. Without pausing her melody, she picked up a stack of napkins and slid them across the table with the precision of a surgeon handing over instruments.

Indro groaned, grabbing the napkins as if they were a lifeline. "I didn't even shake it," he muttered. "It's like the protein staged a coup."

Tasha glanced at the spreading puddle, her humming punctuated by a faint chuckle. "Perhaps it's a performance protest. 'Why didn't you mix me?'"

Indro dabbed furiously at the spill, his ears reddening. "What is it with you and performance art? Not everything is profound. Sometimes it's just inconvenient."

"Spoken like a man betrayed by his own beverage," Tasha said, finally breaking off her humming. She leaned back in her chair, watching him with an air of detached amusement. "You know, this wouldn't happen if you embraced a proper post-workout routine. Maybe even shake your shaker once in a while."

Indro shot her a mock glare. "Next you'll be telling me to journal my feelings about it."

She tilted her head thoughtfully. "Not a bad idea. 'Day 42: The protein betrayed me.' It's practically poetry."

As he worked to mop up the mess, Indro couldn't help but marvel at how unruffled she was, humming her way through the chaos as if it were part of the café's ambiance. It struck him, not for the first time, how Tasha had a knack for absorbing life's absurdities without letting them touch her core. She was the eye of the storm, steady and quietly amused, while the rest of the world flailed around her.

"Why aren't you more flustered?" he asked, half in wonder, half in exasperation.

Tasha shrugged, folding the last napkin with care. "You've seen Mumbai, Indro. If I let every spilled drink or honked horn get to me, I'd have moved to the Himalayas years ago."

Indro sat back, his calculations momentarily forgotten. "And what would you do there? Meditate with monks?"

"Or teach them how to hum Auld Lang Syne," she replied, her grin widening.

He smiled despite himself, the absurdity of the moment settling into something almost comforting. As the last napkin soaked up the remnants of the spill, he realized that with Tasha's steady presence, even a table covered in unshaken protein dregs felt a little less chaotic—and a lot more manageable.

Their shared silence was interrupted by the unmistakable chorus of exaggerated gratitude erupting from the counter. A trio of women, armed with oversized sunglasses and the kind of tans that suggested either a beach or a dedicated tanning booth, had just finished their orders. Their voices rose in synchronized delight, addressing the shy barista with what could only be described as operatic enthusiasm.

"THANK YOU!" declared the leader, her accent teetering precariously between Upper East Side and Mayfair.

The barista flushed, clearly unaccustomed to such attention, as the second woman chimed in with a saccharine, "Thank you SO much!" so dripping with sincerity it seemed on the verge of drowning in its own excess.

Patrons turned to watch, some visibly startled by the display. "Are we witnessing a gratitude competition?" Indro whispered.

"They're not thanking him," Tasha said, taking a measured sip of her espresso. "They're auditioning for sainthood."

"And succeeding," Indro added. "Though their volume control could use some divine intervention."

The trio, apparently satisfied with their performance, departed with a flourish, leaving behind an air of bemusement and the lingering suspicion that their next stop might be a TED Talk on the art of over-thanking.

Indro and Tasha settled into a new more privately placed table just as a bespectacled man at the corner began what could only be described as a hostile corporate takeover of the café. His laptop screen glowed ominously, flanked by a fortress of documents, three empty coffee cups, and a tote bag occupying the next chair with all the entitlement of a monarch. As if that weren't enough, his phone blared an endless stream of notifications loud enough to rival the café's jazz playlist.

"Does he think he's at a WeWork?" Indro muttered, glaring at the man's expanding empire. "I bet he charges himself rent for that corner."

Tasha smirked, sipping her espresso. "Maybe he's conducting an experiment in territorial behavior. Call NatGeo; they'd love this."

Their attention shifted as the man waved at a waiter, gesturing toward an untouched pastry on a neighboring table. "Is this taken?" he asked loudly, without waiting for a response before adding the croissant to his growing pile.

Indro raised an eyebrow. "If he takes one more thing, the café might start charging him property tax."

The man continued obliviously, oblivious to patrons eyeing the dwindling seating options. Tasha leaned forward.

"You should offer him your protein shaker. That might scare him off."

"Or recruit him for my team," Indro quipped. "He's clearly mastered asset acquisition."

As the bespectacled man's empire grew—he had now commandeered a second table, complete with another chair for his tote bag's expanding influence—Tasha leaned back, her gaze drifting toward a flicker of movement near the café counter.

A small, scruffy kitten with fur the color of oversteeped tea padded cautiously into view. Its oversized ears twitched as it surveyed the café, its tiny nose sniffing at the air with the diligence of a connoisseur. The kitten approached cautiously, weaving between chair legs and ignoring the occasional half-hearted shooing from patrons.

"Look at that," Tasha murmured, her tone a mixture of amusement and affection. "Another uninvited guest making themselves at home."

Indro followed her gaze, watching as the kitten sidled up to their table, its tail flicking with the nonchalance of a seasoned trespasser. It paused, looking up at them with wide, expectant eyes. "And what's this one called?" Indro asked, already knowing the answer.

"Nugget," Tasha declared with certainty, reaching down to scoop up the kitten. It didn't protest, curling into her lap as though it had been there all along.

"Nugget," Indro echoed, his tone laced with dry humor. "Every cat you meet is Nugget. Do they know they're part of a collective?"

"All treasures are," Tasha replied serenely, stroking the kitten's tiny head. "Besides, he looks like a Nugget. Don't you, little one?"

Nugget purred in agreement, its contentment vibrating through Tasha's lap. A waiter appeared at that moment, balancing a tray of drinks. Without hesitation, Tasha ordered a small bowl of milk, her tone so decisive that the waiter didn't even blink.

"You're indulging him already," Indro said, watching as the kitten licked a paw with the air of royalty. "Next, you'll be ordering him a croissant."

"Don't tempt me," Tasha replied. "At least Nugget appreciates the simple things."

The milk arrived, and Tasha set the bowl on the table, holding it steady as Nugget leaned forward to lap it up delicately. Indro observed the scene with a faint smile, a flicker of warmth tugging at his usually guarded expression.

"You know," he said after a pause, "I used to rescue birds with my aunts when I was a kid. We'd find them in cages, take them in, and care for them until they were strong enough to fly again."

Tasha glanced up, her hand still resting lightly on Nugget. "That's… unexpected. Why didn't you ever tell me?"

Indro shrugged, his voice softer than usual. "Didn't seem relevant. Besides, it's nice to see someone else with the same instinct. Even if it's… for Nuggets."

The kitten finished its milk and settled back onto Tasha's lap, its small body rising and falling with each sleepy breath. Tasha resumed stroking its fur, her expression unreadable but peaceful. "You're better at this than you let on," she said, her voice gentle.

Tasha leaned back, her gaze wandering toward the toddler with the tablet, now deeply engrossed in the animated squirrel saga. The high-pitched squeals of rodents mid-heist had a persistence that could rival Mumbai's traffic. "Speaking of plots," she began, her tone conversational but laced with dry humor, "I've been using this app for visually impaired people. It connects them with sighted volunteers for assistance."

Indro, absently tapping his pen on his notebook, glanced up. "How does it work?"

"They call when they need help—reading labels, finding objects, navigating unfamiliar spaces," Tasha explained, her voice carrying the kind of understated passion she reserved for topics close to her heart. "You guide them via video. It's simple, but effective."

"Sounds great in theory," Indro said, tilting his head skeptically. "But doesn't it have... let's say, a vulnerability to human creativity? Someone's bound to misuse it."

Tasha nodded, her expression contemplative. "Yesterday, someone asked for color advice on a painting. That was fine. But then he started asking me to describe his surroundings— what the park looked like, whether the birds were flying overhead. It felt... odd. Like he wasn't visually impaired at all."

Indro raised an eyebrow. "So, what did you do?"

"I stayed on the call," Tasha admitted, her tone measured. "Because what if he was genuine? I couldn't risk disconnecting."

Indro set down his napkin with deliberate care, his usual sarcasm giving way to a more serious concern. "Tasha, you can't just trust everyone. There's a line between being helpful and being taken advantage of."

"Trust isn't binary," she replied, her voice calm but firm. "It's nuanced. You can't reduce people to categories like 'trustworthy' or 'not.' Most fall somewhere in between."

Indro leaned back in his chair, his skepticism intact. "Nuance is great in theory, but it's also how scams happen. Numbers, at least, don't pull stunts. They add up, or they don't."

"And people aren't numbers," Tasha countered, her tone softening but gaining an edge of conviction. "That's why you need me to keep you balanced. Otherwise, you'd treat every situation like an equation."

Indro opened his mouth to retort but paused, her words settling over him like an unwelcome yet oddly comforting truth. The café's chaos swirled around them—squirrels squealed, chairs scraped, and a man at the next table loudly negotiated coffee-to-go as though it were a corporate merger—but their table felt momentarily detached from it all.

Tasha's expression softened. "You've always wanted everything to be predictable, haven't you? That's why you're good with numbers—they play by the rules."

"Not always," Indro muttered, thinking of rogue algorithms and uncooperative spreadsheets. "But at least they don't pretend to be birds in a park."

Tasha laughed lightly, a sound that cut through the clamor like a balm. "Maybe that's why I like people. They surprise you, for better or worse."

Indro glanced down at his notebook, where half-finished calculations stared back at him like an unspoken challenge. Somewhere in his chest, a small but persistent voice whispered that maybe, just maybe, Tasha's view of the world had its merits. He silenced it for now, but the thought lingered.

The toddler's tablet reached its climax—animated squirrels breaking into what appeared to be a heavily fortified nut vault—and Indro muttered under his breath, "If squirrels can outsmart a vault, maybe people can outsmart me too."

Tasha smiled, watching him wrestle with the idea, and the distance between them filled.

The barista's voice echoed across the café, clear and commanding: "James Bond!"

Heads swivelled like synchronized swimmers. A man in sunglasses and an unbuttoned blazer rose slowly, pausing just long enough to ensure every pair of eyes was upon him. He strolled to the counter with a confidence so theatrical it deserved its own applause track.

"License to sip?" Tasha murmured, keeping her gaze on her espresso.

"License to overact," Indro muttered, watching as the man collected his latte with a flourish, saluted the barista, and pivoted dramatically toward the exit.

"Do you think he's on a secret mission?" Tasha asked.

"Probably to find a warmer coffee. That latte's been sitting there long enough to apply for citizenship," Indro quipped.

The man's departure left a ripple of bemused silence in his wake, broken only by a nearby patron who muttered, "What's next? Sherlock Holmes ordering chai?"

The restroom door opened, releasing a woman in athleisure who emerged as though stepping off a fashion runway. Behind her, the line of waiting patrons wore expressions ranging from despair to mild homicide.

"She's been in there so long, I think she remodelled," Indro whispered, nudging Tasha.

"Or turned it into an Airbnb," Tasha replied. "Someone should check if she's left a forwarding address."

Just as another patron began to step inside, the woman spun around. "Actually, I forgot my bag!" She darted back in, leaving the queue frozen in collective disbelief. Moments later, muffled sounds of zippers and rustling confirmed that she was, indeed, rearranging her luggage.

Indro shook his head. "This isn't a restroom. It's a transit hub."

"Next she'll be hosting interviews," Tasha added, watching as the queue shifted impatiently.

When the woman finally emerged—for the second time—she offered a breezy "Thanks for waiting!" before disappearing into the café. The queue groaned in unison as the next patron entered, emerging moments later with a look of vague triumph.

The café door swung open to admit Reena—now calling herself Anya—draped in flowing cotton and silver jewelry that jingled softly as she moved. Her entrance had the practiced ease of someone who had never been told to "wait for the next available table."

"Indro!" she exclaimed, sliding into the empty chair as though it had been reserved for her. "Fifteen years, and you're still spilling things?"

"I like to keep my skills sharp," Indro replied dryly, as Tasha raised an eyebrow, clearly intrigued.

"And you," Reena said, turning to Tasha with an air of appraisal, "must be the person keeping him in check."

"Let's call it a work in progress," Tasha replied lightly.

Before Reena could respond, Ranjan entered, his fedora tilted at an angle that suggested both style and effortlessness. He gestured to the table. "Mind if I join? You all look... compelling."

Indro shook his hand. "Pull up a chair. We're discussing the mysteries of life, like why people put sugar in green tea."

"Or call themselves James Bond for a latte," Ranjan added, settling in.

By the counter, an influencer stood poised like a statue, her latte raised in a reverent salute to an invisible audience. She adjusted her cape with the finesse of a magician preparing a grand reveal and tilted her head in an expression so pained it seemed she was contemplating the meaning of life—or at least, the lighting. Her assistants fluttered about like moths around a flame. One balanced a ring light precariously on the counter, while the other wielded a portable fan aimed at her hair, which fluttered obediently in the artificial breeze.

"She's been at it so long, I think her coffee's entered a new tax bracket," Indro muttered, watching as the latte cooled to room temperature under the glare of the ring light.

Tasha chuckled, stirring her espresso. "The latte's the real protagonist here. She's just a supporting character."

The influencer's dedication to her craft—or what passed for it—knew no bounds. When she disappeared into the restroom for what appeared to be a costume change, her assistant blocked the door like a bouncer, hissing at patrons, "Just five more minutes!"

"Five more minutes?" Indro said under his breath. "She's treating the restroom like it's a green room."

"Or a dressing room for an intergalactic fashion show," Reena added, as they both watched the line of waiting patrons grow increasingly mutinous.

Moments later, the restroom door swung open, and the influencer emerged resplendent in a sequined jumpsuit that sparkled aggressively under the café's subdued lighting.

She returned to the deck, where her assistant resumed their post with the fan, directing gusts of air that seemed more appropriate for a monsoon.

"This," the influencer declared dramatically, latte in hand, "is balance."

"Balance?" Tasha whispered to Indro. "Between foam and overconfidence?"

"Or between her coffee and hypothermia," Reena replied.

The influencer's session ended as suddenly as it had begun, leaving the café in a state of mild disrepair. Tables bore the remnants of props, the restroom glistened ominously, and the barista—now back at the counter—looked like he had aged five years in the last thirty minutes.

The conversation, like a pigeon navigating Mumbai traffic, took a sudden turn into the territory of absurdity. "What's your take on chai tea lattes?" Tasha asked, her expression a mix of genuine curiosity and barely suppressed mirth.

"Linguistic absurdity," Indro declared, with the gravity of a man unearthing the Rosetta Stone. "Chai means tea. So, 'chai tea' is tea tea. And 'chai tea latte'? Tea tea with milk. It's the beverage equivalent of saying, 'Please pass me that wet water.'" Reena chimed in, waving her hand dismissively. "Every time I hear it, I feel like asking, 'Would you like your redundant tea with a side of redundant repetition?'"

"Like 'naan bread,'" Tasha said, nodding solemnly, her eyes twinkling.

"'PIN number' is my personal favorite," Indro added dryly. "Just in case we forget that the 'N' already stands for 'number.'"

Reena leaned forward, eyes gleaming. "Oh, that reminds me. At the NCPA during my play's interval, someone asked their companion, 'Do you think they use air-conditioned air here?' I mean, darling, as opposed to what—non-air-conditioned air trapped in a tiny time capsule?"

Ranjan chuckled. "And I remember staying for the second act purely because I thought the play might explain the logic behind that question."

"You stayed," Reena said archly, "because you thought existential dialogue would improve your conversational repertoire."

"I stayed," Ranjan corrected, smirking, "because the plot twists were more intricate than your scarf."

Indro, observing the exchange, shook his head. "The English language doesn't stand a chance with this crowd."

As the laughter settled, the topic drifted, buoyed by the relaxed camaraderie of shared absurdity. "What about you, Indro?" Tasha asked, her tone softening into curiosity. "Any hidden talents? Anything that doesn't involve muttering about spreadsheets or glaring at people who hog restrooms?"

Indro hesitated, caught off-guard. He tapped his fingers on the table, the rhythm uncharacteristically uncertain. "I wanted to learn guitar once," he admitted, his voice quieter now. "But it didn't fit the IIT-IIM roadmap."

Tasha tilted her head, her expression thoughtful. "Why didn't anyone encourage you?"

"It didn't seem… relevant," Indro said, his words falling into the quiet like pebbles into a pond.

Tasha's brow furrowed slightly, a rare flicker of indignation crossing her face. "Relevance is overrated," she said, her voice firm but kind. "You're more than projections and spreadsheets, you know."

Ranjan, ever the opportunist, leaned forward with a grin. "I can see it now—Indro Sen, lead guitarist of 'Equity & Strings.' The crowd goes wild as you shred the intro to Balance Sheets Blues."

The group dissolved into laughter again, the levity of Ranjan's jesting a welcome counterpoint to the weight of Indro's admission.

Tasha leaned back, her gaze turning toward the sea, where the waves seemed to roll with an effortless rhythm. "The thing about hidden talents," she mused, "is that they're never really lost. Just waiting for the right moment to be rediscovered."

"Like Mumbai's infrastructure," Indro quipped, unable to resist.

"Except your talents might actually be functional," Tasha shot back, the corners of her mouth lifting in a grin.

Ranjan gestured toward the sea, his grin infectious. "To Mumbai—its chaos, its jazz, and its unbothered cats."

"To better manners," Tasha added, her smile knowing.

"And coffee that actually gets drunk," Indro said with a smirk.

Their mugs clinked softly, carrying the echoes of humor, humanity, and the charm of shared absurdity into the night.

Chapter 4

Mastery Over Morning Fate

The morning light draped Marine Drive in a golden haze, the sea sparkling as if it had polished itself overnight for an audience that would never arrive. Indro adjusted his glasses, holding his protein shaker tightly, its contents sloshing gently with each step. His sneakers, pristine and white, gleamed with an optimism entirely unsuited to Mumbai's streets.

Tasha joined him near NCPA, her emerald-green jumpsuit adorned with flamingos that looked mildly scandalized by the city's chaos. She fell into step with practiced ease, her gait purposeful yet unhurried.

"White sneakers. Again," she remarked, her tone teetering between admiration and mockery. "You do realize this city is actively plotting against them."

"They survived yesterday," Indro said, defensively. "It's called discipline."

"It's called denial," Tasha quipped, adjusting her sunglasses. "But hey, live your truth."

Indro adjusted his glasses, gripping his protein shaker with the wary caution of a man guarding a fragile secret. Each slosh of its contents echoed his determination to fortify himself against Mumbai's microbial offerings. "Immune fortification," he muttered, more to himself than anyone else, as though the shaker were a talisman against the city's unpredictable hygiene.

They walked in companionable silence for a moment, the promenade around them coming to life. Joggers pounded the pavement with varying degrees of determination, while post-party stragglers, still glittering from last night, meandered like lost moths. The air carried a mix of salt, exhaust, and the faintly tragic undertone of regret.

Ahead, a garbage truck lumbered along, its battered body groaning under the weight of Mumbai's excesses. A trail of liquid seeped ominously from its overfilled belly, leaving a pungent trail that glistened in the morning light. The truck honked with theatrical urgency, its tone somewhere between a battle cry and a complaint.

Indro sidestepped instinctively as the liquid came perilously close to his sneakers. "Is that… leaking? Shouldn't there be a law against that?"

"There is," Tasha said, watching the sanitation worker perched on the truck's edge, gazing at them, through them, beyond them. "But the truck didn't read it." Watching the garbage truck lumbering past, leaving its trail of ominous liquid, Indro's enthusiasm for finishing his shake waned dramatically. He glanced at the dregs swirling in his shaker, now resembling something less like a health drink and more like a petri dish in training. "Discipline," he murmured unconvincingly, raising the shaker halfway to his lips before lowering it again with a sigh.

A cab pulled alongside them, its passenger leaning out of the window with cheeks puffed like a trumpet player mid-performance. Before they could react, a crimson arc sailed through the air, landing with an audible splat just inches from Indro's sneakers.

He froze, his face a study in restrained horror. Tasha, remarkably composed, adjusted her sunglasses. "Mumbai: where you don't need permission to perform."

"That," Indro said tightly, "is why I believe in karma."

"Funny," Tasha said, "because I think karma just spit at you."

The sun rose higher as they walked toward Chowpatty, the city unfolding its peculiar brand of resilience around them. Near the tetrapods, Tasha paused, her gaze fixed on the undulating waves. Indro frowned at the plastic bottles wedged among the concrete forms, their glinting surfaces mocking the sea's attempts to reclaim its dignity.

"Do you ever think about astrology?" Tasha asked suddenly. Indro paused mid-step, adjusting his glasses with the air of a man preparing to debunk a particularly elaborate hoax. "Only when my relatives corner me into downloading apps with names like 'Zodiac Master 3000.'"

Tasha stifled a laugh. "So, you're a skeptic."

"Skeptic?" Indro scoffed. "I prefer 'realist.' Stars are great for navigation, not career advice. I mean, what's a constellation supposed to know about quarterly projections?"

"They don't," Tasha replied, her tone unruffled. "Astrology isn't about answers. It's about comfort. Therapy disguised as constellations."

"Comfort?" Indro said, incredulous. "I already have that. Weighted blankets, thank you very much."

"Weighted blankets?" Tasha repeated, her brow arching.

Indro straightened defensively. "They're scientifically proven to reduce anxiety. Unlike horoscopes, which—let's face it—are just cosmic Mad Libs."

"Maybe," Tasha mused, "but horoscopes are a cheap placebo. Weighted blankets cost a fortune and make you look like you're training for a medieval joust."

"Training for better sleep," Indro corrected, clutching his protein shaker like a shield. "And at least my blanket doesn't pretend to predict my future."

"No," Tasha admitted, "but it probably wouldn't object if someone did."

Indro tilted his head. "Do you actually believe in all this?"

"I believe in moments of clarity," Tasha said, watching the waves lap against the tetrapods. "Sometimes, when the stars align—or when someone says the right thing—it helps."

"Helps what?" Indro asked, his tone softening.

"Helps make sense of things," Tasha replied, a faint smile playing on her lips. "Not everything needs to add up like one of your spreadsheets."

"Spreadsheets are honest," Indro muttered, though without conviction.

"People aren't numbers," Tasha said simply. "And neither are stars."

"Still, I'd trust data over stars."

"Of course you would," Tasha replied. "You're all about destinations. I prefer the journey."

As their conversation drifted toward an agreeable lull, a woman in a cerulean sari approached the edge of the promenade with a dramatic air that suggested she was about to alter the course of history—or at least her morning. In her hand, she clutched a small, bundled offering wrapped in shimmering fabric, which she flung toward the waves with a fervor that could have rivaled an Olympic discus thrower.

The bundle arced gracefully through the air, then landed with a dull thud directly atop the tetrapods, unfurling to reveal what looked like petals, grains, and something metallic. The trio paused, their expressions somewhere between bemusement and resignation.

"Beautiful form," Indro observed dryly. "Shame about the execution."

"Perhaps the tetrapods weren't part of her plan," Tasha suggested, her tone betraying no small amount of amusement.

"But then again, in Mumbai, nothing ever lands where you intend it to."

The bundle sat there, undeterred, glinting in the sunlight like an abstract sculpture. Around it, other similar offerings had also claimed the tetrapods, turning the concrete structures into a peculiar collage of tradition, improvisation, and unintended permanence.

"You'd think someone might have considered designing something to catch these before they pile up," Indro said, adjusting his glasses. "An offering chute. Or maybe a delivery service—'Throw it, and we'll make sure it actually reaches the sea.'"

Tasha chuckled. "We could combine it with the city's other great oversight: pets. Offer a double-duty service. Drop your biodegradable offering and dispose of your dog's morning business while you're at it."

Indro smirked. "Two birds, one stone. Or rather, two responsibilities, one bin."

A jogger passed by with a lively golden retriever in tow, its leash taut as the dog sniffed enthusiastically at every possible surface. The jogger slowed down long enough to glance apologetically at a spot the retriever had freshly claimed as its own—and then sped up without so much as a backward glance.

"Ah," Indro said, his tone almost reverent, "the great unsung heroes of the promenade: unclaimed deposits."

"You can't blame the dogs," Tasha replied. "It's not their fault they've got no support staff."

Indro raised an eyebrow. "Support staff? You mean owners with bags?"

"Exactly," Tasha said, her lips twitching. "But who has the time? In Mumbai, we're all too busy throwing things we can't be bothered to pick up."

As the morning sun climbed higher, they moved on, leaving the tetrapods to their eclectic gallery of unintended installations and the promenade to its bustling exhibition of unfiltered humanity.

Max joined them near Chowpatty, coconut in hand and camera slung casually over his shoulder. His grin was wide and unguarded, a rarity in a city that thrived on guarded expressions. "Morning!" Max called out, happy to see his uncle Indro, raising his coconut like a toast. "Bright-eyed and bushy-tailed?"

"More like cautiously caffeinated," Tasha replied, nodding toward his camera. "You've been busy, I see."

"Documenting the chaos," Max said, tapping the lens. "It's like every corner of this city is staging its own performance."

"Careful," Indro quipped, "the city charges royalties for metaphors."

Max grinned, taking a sip. "Well, I've survived the train, dodged a dozen cabs, and even made friends with a stray dog. I think I'm officially one of you."

"Not quite," Tasha said. "Your optimism's still intact. Give it time."

"And a few more laundry splashes," Indro added. "That'll do the trick."

Max laughed, shifting the coconut to his other hand. "Mumbai's like an initiation ritual, isn't it? Tough at first, but then it gets under your skin."

"More like a houseguest who never leaves," Tasha said. "Annoying, but oddly endearing."

They sat people watching for a bit. "That movie," Tasha began, her tone reflective, "the one with the platform and the food—isn't it just gratuitous? All gore, no nuance."

"It's a metaphor," Indro said, shrugging. "A bit on the nose, but it makes its point."

"It's disturbing for the sake of it," Tasha countered. "Doesn't need to shove its moral into your face like a fist."

"Sometimes you need the fist," Indro replied. "People don't listen otherwise."

"Or maybe they listen better when it's subtle," Tasha argued. "You're all about the direct route, but life's more winding."

"Winding leads to getting lost," Indro said, adjusting his glasses. "Straight roads get you there faster."

Tasha's grin was faint but amused. "And yet you're the one who always stops to comment on the scenery."

Max, sipping his coconut, observed them both. "You two need a podcast."

Near the southern end of Marine Drive, a cleaning truck rumbled into view, its brushes whirring industriously. Two sanitation workers followed it with brooms, sweeping up what the machine missed.

Indro paused to watch the scene; his expression curious. "So, the machine cleans, and they… clean what's already clean?"

"It's a tag team," Tasha said, smirking. "Man versus machine, Mumbai edition."

Max adjusted his camera, snapping a picture. "It's like they don't trust the machine."

"Or maybe the machine doesn't trust them," Indro suggested. "We should get them into couples therapy."

One of the workers waved cheerfully at them, his broom slashing through a pile of leaves with the determination of a swordsman. "Good morning, saab!"

"Good morning!" Tasha called back. "Love the teamwork."

"By noon, all clean!" the man promised, though his partner looked less convinced.

"By noon," Indro muttered as they walked on, "Mumbai's optimism will never die."

They passed a public toilet near the beach, its bold blue facade a testament to civic optimism. The stench that emanated from it, however, was less optimistic. A lone figure squatted by the rocks nearby, his choice of location a clear rejection of the facility's promises.

"Why not use the toilet?" Max asked, wrinkling his nose.

"Public toilets here are like old elevators," Tasha said. "Everyone assumes they'll collapse the moment you trust them."

"And the sea's free," Indro added. "Not hygienic, but free."

Just past Chowpatty, as they strolled beneath the shadow of a weathered high-rise, the unmistakable rustle of something descending through the air caught their attention. A crumpled packet of chips sailed downward, spinning lazily, before landing a few feet away with a lacklustre plop.

"Ah," Indro said, gesturing grandly, "Mumbai's newest art installation. Abstract littering."

Tasha bent down, picking up the packet with the same care one might reserve for handling a venomous creature. "I'm amazed at the precision. Do you think they're training for Olympic freefall littering?"

"Trash cans," Indro mused, "are clearly considered a bourgeois relic. The open air, however? Timeless."

Max, sipping his coconut, chimed in. "It's efficiency. If gravity's doing the work, why not let it handle the cleanup too?"

Nugget, weaving around Tasha's ankles, sniffed the discarded packet disdainfully before flicking her tail in silent judgment.

"You know," Tasha said, tossing the packet into a nearby bin, "I read somewhere that littering is sometimes a quiet form of rebellion. A way for people to reject rules that feel irrelevant or imposed."

Indro looked at her, incredulous. "And here I was thinking it was just laziness with a side of apathy."

"Rebellion," Max said, thoughtfully staring up at the high-rise. "But without follow-through. It's like crime, if crime had no stakes."

Nugget leapt gracefully onto a nearby ledge, curling her tail neatly around her paws. She cast a critical eye up at the building, as if daring the culprit to try again. Indro pointed at her approvingly. "Even the cat's unimpressed. A true connoisseur of etiquette."

Tasha grinned, wiping her hands theatrically on her jumpsuit. "I think we can all agree that Nugget should be running this city."

Max raised his coconut in salute. "To Nugget, arbiter of civic manners."

They laughed, the odd mix of exasperation and amusement only Mumbai could inspire carrying them forward along the promenade.

Further along, a bespectacled man in a crisp white kurta joined them, tossing handfuls of grain to a frenzy of pigeons. The birds descended with military precision; their cooing almost triumphant.

"Joshi," Tasha greeted him warmly. "Still feeding the unsanitary masses?"

"It's karma," Joshi replied, unbothered. "You should try it. Builds character."

"Spreads diseases," Tasha countered. "Histoplasmosis, cryptococcosis—it's practically a biohazard."

Joshi chuckled. "Madam, if pigeons disappear, the balance tips. You'll see."

"Balance looks messy," Max observed, snapping a photo of the chaos.

"Like life," Joshi said with a smile. He wiggled his toes, spreading the grains with ambidextrousness. "Barefoot is freedom," he announced.

Max, resplendent in neon green Crocs, raised an eyebrow. "Freedom is overrated. Protection is where it's at."

Indro glanced at his sneakers, gleaming valiantly despite their perilous journey. "And protection," he added dryly, "comes with maintenance. Ever tried rescuing white sneakers from garbage truck juice?"

Joshi chuckled, holding out his grain-filled hand. "All this fuss, and yet we step on the same ground."

"Some of us step smarter," Max whispered to Tasha, wiggling his Crocs-covered foot. "Fashion, function, and forgiveness—all in one."

After parting ways with Joshi, they encountered a vegetable vendor setting up near a drain. Carrots and cabbages formed orderly piles, their vibrancy at odds with the murky liquid gurgling nearby. A goat inspected the display, nibbling a cabbage leaf before walking away in apparent disappointment.

"Breakfast options?" Tasha asked, pointing at the carrots.

"I'll take the one with cholera," Indro replied dryly. The moment arrived when discipline met its ultimate foe. As they passed the drain, Indro stumbled, his shaker slipping from his grasp. It landed with a muted thud, perilously close to the murky stream gurgling nearby. He froze, his pristine sneakers rooted to the ground in horror.

Tasha's eyebrows lifted. "And there goes your immunity booster."

Indro gingerly picked up the shaker, holding it at arm's length as though it were evidence from a crime scene. "No dustbins," he muttered helplessly. "The city's greatest unsolved mystery."

As the group meandered along, a sudden splash startled them. A torrent of water from freshly wrung clothes fell from a high balcony, narrowly missing Indro's sneakers but drenching a confused Nugget, who had been prowling close by.

Nugget leapt with the grace of a prima ballerina onto Max's shoulder, her fur a soggy mess. She glared up at the offending balcony, her tail flicking in indignation.

"Another miracle of urban planning," Indro muttered, shaking droplets from his glasses.

Max offered Nugget a tissue, earning a disdainful sniff. "Do people think gravity doesn't exist?" he asked.

"It's selective," Tasha said. "Applies to everyone except people with balconies."

"Or maybe they think Mumbai's sidewalks are self-cleaning," Indro added. "Innovative, really."

The group fell into laughter, their camaraderie softening the absurdity of the moment.

By the time they reached the bakery, Indro was still clutching the shaker with visible reluctance. Max grinned at him, sipping his coconut. "New accessory, Indro? Very avant-garde."

"It's called responsibility," Indro retorted. "Unlike the balcony drip irrigation system back there."

Inside the bakery, they squeezed into a corner table, their laughter mingling with the hum of conversation.

"This place," Max said, tearing into a bun, "makes it all worth it."

"It always does," Tasha said, sipping her chai. "Even the chaos."

Indro raised his cup. "To resilience. And clean sneakers."

Their toast was met with Nugget's indignant yowl, a fitting conclusion to another morning in the city of dreams.

Chapter 5

Mastery in the Marketplace

Mumbai, as Tasha often declared, was a city with a personality disorder. It couldn't decide if it wanted to be a bustling metropolis or a treasure chest of eccentricities. The streets were both its arteries and its battlegrounds, where rickshaws and SUVs waged silent wars, and pedestrians darted through traffic with the agility of seasoned gladiators.

"Why am I here?" Indro asked, his tone as flat as the stale vada pav he had once been tricked into eating.

Tasha, marching ahead with the determination of an explorer seeking El Dorado, didn't bother to turn around. "Because your apartment looks like a hospital waiting room, and I have a reputation to maintain."

"My apartment is minimalist," Indro protested.

"Your apartment," Tasha countered, "has all the personality of an Excel spreadsheet."

Indro sighed, sidestepping a handcart piled high with crates of mangoes. "Why can't I just order a lamp online like a normal person?"

"Because" Tasha replied, stopping abruptly in front of a particularly chaotic alley, "a lamp isn't just a lamp. It's the soul of a room."

"I was under the impression that was the role of, you know, people," Indro muttered. He changed the topic, eagerly showing her his brand-new protein shaker, the chrome lid gleaming under the shop's dim light. "Look at this beauty," he said, holding it aloft.

Tasha raised an eyebrow. "Another one? You're collecting gym accessories like stamps."

"It's not just a shaker," Indro replied. "It's ergonomically designed, double-insulated, and... functional."

"Functional?" Tasha teased. "It looks like you're carrying a trophy for Most Improved Biceps."

"Mock all you want," Indro said, unscrewing the lid to demonstrate. "This is engineering excellence."

Tasha ignored him, pointing dramatically to a sign hanging precariously above a narrow doorway. Zahid's Antiques—Wonders Await.

"Wonders, huh?" Indro said, raising an eyebrow. "Sounds like the tagline for a scam."

"Don't be so cynical," Tasha said, grabbing his arm and dragging him toward the shop. "This is Mumbai. Wonders are everywhere. You just must be brave enough to look for them."

Stepping into Zahid's Antiques felt like entering a magician's lair, where every object carried a spell. Dust motes pirouetted in shafts of light streaming through a stained-glass window, casting patterns on shelves groaning under the weight of history. Brass lamps sat next to ancient binoculars, and a stack of yellowed Bollywood magazines formed a precarious tower in one corner. Perched atop it all, surveying its kingdom, was a Persian cat with a tail so plume-like it might have doubled as an imperial fan in another life.

"Nawab," Zahid called, emerging from behind a shelf laden with clocks all ticking at different tempos. "Don't frighten the guests."

The cat, unperturbed, flicked its tail and resumed its regal pose.

Zahid himself was as much a relic as his shop: an aging man in a spotless kurta, his salt-and-pepper beard trimmed with care, and eyes that glinted with a lifetime of stories. He looked at Tasha and Indro with a mix of curiosity and amusement.

"Welcome," he said warmly. "Are you here for wonders, history, or just to make friends with my Nawab?"

"Definitely here for wonders," Tasha said, crouching down to greet the cat. "Hello, Nugget. Aren't you the most royal of cats?"

Zahid frowned. "His name is Nawab, ma'am. Please, don't insult his lineage."

But Nawab—or Nugget, as Tasha promptly renamed him—had already melted under her gentle touch, purring with the kind of self-satisfied rumble only a cat can manage.

"She has a way with cats," Indro muttered. "And apparently, no respect for their identities."

As Zahid led them toward the shelves, he gestured grandly toward a peculiar lamp shaped like a sand dune, its brass surface etched with intricate ripples. "This, my friends," Zahid announced, "is inspired by the desert. A piece of art and resilience."

Tasha paused, intrigued. "It's very Dune-like."

Zahid's eyes sparkled. "Ah, a fan of the desert epic! Dune—an unparalleled exploration of power, survival, and the human spirit."

"Frank Herbert was brilliant," Tasha agreed. "But I don't think Tolkien would've approved. He famously disliked allegories, especially ones as blatant as Dune's political metaphors."

Zahid raised an eyebrow. "And yet Tolkien spent thousands of words describing trees. Surely, a bit of political intrigue wouldn't hurt?"

Tasha laughed. "Tolkien's worlds are timeless. He believed in the organic stories that grow naturally, rooted in the eternal struggles of good and evil. Dune, on the other hand, is all about power dynamics."

"Power is eternal," Zahid said, tapping the lamp. "Just like this piece. It may look fragile, but it's designed to endure."

Indro, who had been quietly studying a clock shaped like a ship's wheel, muttered, "Honestly, this is why I stick to spreadsheets. No debates, just numbers."

Tasha glanced at him, her lips twitching. "Careful, Indro. That sounds dangerously close to an allegory."

As Zahid led them deeper into the shop, Tasha explained their mission. "We're looking for a floor lamp—for his apartment, not mine."

"Something stylish but understated," Indro added. "Functional, not too flashy."

Zahid's eyes sparkled. "Ah, you want a lamp with soul. I have just the thing." He rummaged through a stack of precariously balanced artifacts and pulled out a brass lamp shaped like a banyan tree; its branches etched with intricate detail.

"This," Zahid declared, "has survived floods, blackouts, and even a Bollywood film shoot. It's perfect."

"Beautiful," Tasha breathed.

"Expensive," Indro observed.

As they haggled over the price, Zahid waxed philosophical about the market's ecosystem. "This lamp, like everything here, wouldn't be in your hands without the handcart pullers. They're the veins of this market, carrying life from one end of the city to the other."

"True," Tasha agreed, "but surely electric carts would make things easier for them?"

Zahid frowned. "Easier, perhaps. But what about the tradition? My father ran this shop with handcart deliveries; his father before him traded spices the same way. Progress is fine, but do we want to replace a legacy with batteries and buttons?"

"And congestion?" Indro countered. "Handcarts slow everything down. They block roads, create bottlenecks…"

Zahid chuckled, leaning on the counter. "Ah, congestion! The great villain of Mumbai. But let me ask you this: would you prefer a 200-year-old cart carrying heritage, or another SUV carrying impatience?"

Their debate was interrupted by the arrival of Haresh, a man with a broad smile and a scarf tied loosely around his neck. He strode in, pushing a cart piled high with goods, his steps sure and his manner easy. He proceeded to park his cart in the shade of a precariously leaning pole. Leaning casually on the handle, he exhaled with the drama of a man who had just climbed Everest.

"Shade," he said, grinning at Indro. "The city's finest five-star amenity."

Tasha shook her head. "Imagine if markets had actual rest zones—benches, shade, maybe a chai stall that doesn't double as a fire hazard."

Haresh chuckled. "And maybe a valet for our carts while you're at it?"

"Next thing you know, there'll be a Michelin rating for foot massage corners."

"City planners don't think about us," Haresh said. "We're like the wiring behind a TV. Everyone uses it, no one sees it."

Tasha frowned. "They should see you. Rest stops would boost efficiency and keep you healthy."

Haresh shrugged with a practiced nonchalance. "Until then, we make do with the shadow of a pole."

"Ah, Haresh!" Zahid exclaimed. "You're just in time. Meet your next delivery—a banyan lamp and two enthusiastic customers."

Haresh took one look at the lamp and nodded. "Light, compared to the marble tiles from last week. That was a workout."

Tasha, intrigued, asked, "Do you ever get tired of pulling carts?"

Haresh shrugged. "Tired? Sometimes. But this work keeps me fit, and it connects me to the city. I'm like Mumbai's veins, pumping goods to where they're needed."

"Also, like veins," Zahid added, "he occasionally gets blocked by potholes."

Everyone laughed as Haresh loaded the lamp onto his cart. Nawab—or Nugget—followed Tasha to the door, rubbing against her legs in a rare display of affection. As Haresh adjusted the straps on his cart, Zahid leaned against the counter. "You know, Tasha, Dune reminds me of this handcart. Layered, essential, and often underestimated."

"Layered chaos, you mean," Indro said, stepping around a stray dog. "Just like Mumbai."

Tasha folded her arms. "Tolkien would disagree. He'd see the handcart as a testament to pastoral simplicity, a symbol of endurance without the machinations of politics."

Haresh looked up, intrigued. "Tolkien? Is that another customer who loves handcarts?"

Tasha laughed. "Not exactly. He's the author of The Lord of the Rings. He believed in the heroism of simple folk—like hobbits."

"Well, I'm no hobbit," Haresh said, flexing his arms, "but I can deliver like one. No ring, though. Just a lamp."

Zahid nodded sagely. "Dune shows us the power of the overlooked. The cart puller is the Fremen of Mumbai, navigating chaos with grace."

Indro smirked. "All this over a cart? Next, you'll be telling me my protein shaker is the One Ring."

"Only if it glows," Tasha replied, grinning.

"Is it just me," Indro began, sniffing suspiciously, "or does this street have... layers?"

Haresh grinned. "Mumbai's signature scent. A little masala, a little history, and yesterday's rainwater."

"Is there even a public restroom nearby?" Tasha asked, grimacing.

Haresh shook his head. "Three lanes down, but nobody uses it. Safer to wait for a downpour."

Indro winced. "So, no wonder your cardio is impeccable. You're running marathons just to find a restroom. Doesn't anyone complain?"

Haresh laughed. "Complain to whom? Potholes don't listen, and pigeons don't care."

"Mumbai's streets are not so much thoroughfares as they are elaborate stage productions. There are the lead performers—the screeching rickshaws and honking taxis—accompanied by an ensemble of pedestrians jaywalking with Olympic determination, and the occasional cow, sauntering across as though it owns the joint. But the unsung heroes of this chaotic ballet are the handcarts: wooden planks on rickety wheels, dragged by men whose sinewy arms seem carved from granite.

Handcarts are Mumbai's oldest logistical marvels, predating not just e-commerce but also electricity. They are the arteries through which the lifeblood of commerce flows—vegetables, steel rods, ancient gramophones, and occasionally, inexplicably, a life-sized cutout of Rajnikanth.

Yet, they remain misunderstood. The average motorist, trapped behind a particularly overloaded cart, sees not a heroic link in the supply chain but an obstacle, a wheeled embodiment of inconvenience." Haresh was eloquent and insightful, and they listened, understanding.

Haresh tipped his scarf in farewell, the cart creaking softly as it rolled away. Zahid watched him go, his expression thoughtful. "In Dune, they say the desert teaches us resilience. These pullers are our navigators, finding paths where none seem possible."

Tasha, still cradling a small lamp she had picked up almost without thought, countered with a smile. "Tolkien would call them heroes of the simple life—doing extraordinary things quietly."

Indro adjusted his glasses. "I'm going to need a glossary for this conversation. Fremen, hobbits… any relatable comparisons?"

Tasha tapped the lamp. "Think of it this way: you're Sauron, the lamp's the Ring, and Zahid is Gandalf."

Zahid straightened, clearly delighted. "I accept this role. Haresh, of course, is Frodo."

"Of course," Indro said, shaking his head. "Now I just need to figure out if I'm supposed to root for the lamp or destroy it."

"Honestly," Indro began, after enough silence had seeped, adjusting his spectacles as he tried to navigate a particularly narrow lane, "these handcarts are like stubborn relatives. You can't get rid of them, and they're always in the way."

Ahead of him, Haresh—the cart-pulling marvel—paused to wipe his brow. The cart behind him groaned under the weight of its load, which appeared to consist of a large brass lamp, several marble tiles, and what might have been half of a dismantled swing set.

"Stubborn, eh?" Haresh said, grinning as he leaned casually on the cart's handle. "That's one way to look at it. But without us, who's going to deliver that shiny lamp of yours? Amazon drones?"

Tasha, striding beside them with her customary enthusiasm, chimed in. "Haresh has a point. These carts have been around for centuries, moving goods through lanes where no vehicle can go. They're part of Mumbai's DNA."

"They're also part of its congestion," Indro retorted, sidestepping a stray cat that appeared to be making its own delivery run. "Look at this road. Double-parked cars, hawkers everywhere, and then a cart like yours, Haresh, trying to squeeze through. It's a logistical nightmare."

Haresh adjusted his scarf, his expression calm. "I've heard worse. One gentleman in a BMW once shouted, 'Why are you even here?' I wanted to tell him, 'Because you don't have the boot space for 200 kilograms of steel rods, my friend.'"

"What about electric carts?" Tasha interjected, her voice brimming with her characteristic mix of optimism and overthinking. "Wouldn't they solve so many problems? Less strain on the pullers, fewer emissions, and they'd move faster."

Haresh chuckled. "They're a fine idea, ma'am. But who's going to pay for them? An electric cart costs three times what this wooden beauty does. And what happens when the battery runs out halfway up Parel? You think the battery charger will show up with a dabbawalla?"

Indro smirked. "He's got a point, Tasha. Economics aside, do you really think Mumbai is ready for electric carts? We don't even have enough charging points for cars."

"Well," Tasha said, undeterred, "progress has to start somewhere. If we invest in infrastructure, maybe—"

"Maybe," Haresh interrupted, "I'll be delivering your electric cart parts on my handcart. It's tradition. My grandfather hauled spices this way. My father hauled fabric. Me? I haul everything from mangoes to marble. If this city has a pulse, it's us pullers who keep it pumping."

"Tradition is all well and good," Indro said, "but what about the toll it takes on you? You're dragging half a ton through streets designed for bicycles. Surely, there are days you wish for something easier."

Haresh's face softened. "Of course. There are days I feel every muscle and every joint. Days when the potholes feel deeper, and the honks sound louder. But there's dignity in this work. When I deliver something, whether it's a box of mangoes or that shiny lamp of yours, I know I've earned my bread."

Tasha, clearly moved, asked, "Do you ever think about stopping?"

"Stopping?" Haresh grinned. "Stopping is for machines, ma'am. Me? I adapt. You learn to nap standing up. You learn to dodge stray dogs. And you learn that even the angriest motorist has to smile when you deliver a stack of laddoos to their wedding."

As Haresh maneuvered his cart onto the road, a scooter whizzed by, missing the edge of the cart by inches. "Oy!" Haresh yelled, shaking his head. "You value your life so little? This lamp's worth more than that ride of yours!"

Indro, dodging another pedestrian, muttered, "every man for himself?"

Haresh laughed. "We who work this way are in a perpetual street cricket match. Everyone's improvising, and no one's following the umpire."

"Dedicated lanes," Indro suggested. "For handcarts. Safer and more efficient."

"Dedicated lanes." Haresh repeated with mock solemnity. "Shall I build them on the Arabian Sea?"

As they reached Indro's apartment, Haresh carefully unloaded the lamp. It gleamed in the fading sunlight, a symbol not just of light but of the stories woven into its journey.

"Here you go," Haresh said, stepping back with a flourish. "One lamp, delivered with a side of unsolicited philosophy."

Tasha handed him a tip, her smile genuine. "Thank you, Haresh. For everything." Haresh's eyes wandered to Indro's shaker. "That's a fancy bottle. What does it do?"

Indro hesitated. "It... shakes my liquid protein, that I've mostly dribbled down my chin on our little adventure, it's empty now."

Haresh's grin widened. "Can I see it?"

Reluctantly, Indro handed it over. Haresh turned it over, examining it like a rare artifact. "Perfect size for lassi," he said appreciatively.

Tasha stifled a grin as Indro rinsed it out and softly sighed, "Fine. Keep it."

Haresh's face lit up. "Thank you, Made my day."

As Haresh disappeared into the thrumming city, Indro turned to Tasha. "You know, I think I finally understand why you love these old things."

"Because they're soulful?"

"No," Indro said, smirking. "Because they're impossible to ignore. Like you."

Tasha laughed, swatting his arm. And as the lamp cast its golden glow, they stood together, listening to the distant creak of a handcart—a sound as old as the city itself, carrying its history and its hopes into the future.

Chapter 6

Mastery By Merchandise

The Colaba Causeway was alive as usual, pulsating with a rhythm that could only be described as uniquely Mumbai. It was a street where the chaos felt not chaotic but rather like a jazz band in full swing, each instrument seemingly doing its own thing, yet somehow managing to stay in tune. Bicycle bells chimed in counterpoint to the cries of vendors, while the occasional honk from an auto-rickshaw provided a jarring crescendo. The air was heavy with the aromas of frying samosas, leather freshly buffed into submission, and a not-insignificant contribution from the city's exhaust pipes, all combining into a fragrance that could charitably be labeled "Mumbai Noir."

Tasha took a deep, enthusiastic sniff of this bouquet, her face alight with the fervor of an evangelist about to deliver a sermon. "This," she announced, gesturing at the bustling street as if she had personally invented it, "is the heartbeat of the city. Raw, unfiltered, unapologetic."

Indro, walking a few paces behind with the air of someone hoping not to be seen in the company of a lunatic, gave her a look of mingled exasperation and resignation. "It's a migraine waiting to happen," he said, sidestepping a wayward cyclist. He glanced down at his shoe, now sporting a distinctly chai-colored stain. "And I think someone's morning tea just had a close encounter with my left loafer."

Tasha, undeterred, gave him a sparkling smile. "Typical," she said, darting toward a stall draped with kaleidoscopic scarves. "You see inconvenience; I see poetry."

"Poetry?" Indro raised an eyebrow. "You mean the guy over there trying to flog a plastic Taj Mahal for two thousand rupees? What's next, a bespoke Gateway of India snow globe?"

Tasha ignored him, her attention already captured by something infinitely more charming. Perched atop a precarious pile of scarves at the nearest stall was an orange tabby cat, gazing at the bustling crowd with the serene indifference of a monarch surveying an assembly of particularly dull courtiers.

"Oh, my goodness," Tasha breathed, her voice a reverent whisper. "Look at him. He's perfect."

The vendor, a stocky man with a neatly trimmed moustache that seemed to quiver with personality, perked up immediately. "Ah, madam," he said, his voice dripping with oily enthusiasm, "you have excellent taste! This scarf—hand-dyed, pure silk. Only 5,000 rupees."

"Not the scarf," Tasha said, already reaching out to scratch the cat's chin. "The cat."

The vendor burst into laughter, a sound that managed to be both theatrical and genuinely amused. "That's Nugget!" he declared, puffing out his chest. "My business partner."

Tasha frowned thoughtfully. "No, no. He's just pretending to be a Nugget. He's definitely the Nugget."

As if to prove her point, the cat stretched languidly, nuzzling her hand and emitting a purr that sounded less like a housecat and more like a well-tuned motorbike. Indro, watching this unfold, heaved a sigh of a man resigned to the inevitable. "We've been here less than five minutes, and you've adopted someone else's cat."

"I didn't adopt him," Tasha corrected, cradling Nugget like he was the K. "He chose me."

The vendor, sensing an opportunity to capitalize on this feline fascination, held up a bright yellow scarf. "For you, madam," he said, "just 4,500 rupees. Very rare. Hand-dyed with turmeric."

"Tasha, don't," Indro warned. "That scarf is about as silk as my protein shake is single malt."

Tasha, however, had already drifted into another train of thought, one that had occupied her mind ever since the Mumbai heat had taken its toll on her olfactory sensibilities. "You know," she said, "what this city really needs is perfume vending machines. Strategic installations across hotspots like Colaba. Imagine—lavender in the morning, sandalwood in the evening, a little citrus for that post-samosa stroll."

Indro groaned. "Please tell me this isn't another one of your entrepreneurial brainstorms."

"Why not?" Tasha said brightly. "I'd call it Scents of Mumbai. The perfumes would use local inspirations. Jasmine, chai, maybe even a dash of sea breeze. You wouldn't have to endure the, er, natural musk of your fellow commuters ever again."

"At least you're sparing me from being turned into your guinea pig this time," Indro muttered, only to glance down and realize he'd inadvertently stepped into a puddle of what he could only hope was water. "For heaven's sake! Why do we not have functional drainage systems?"

Tasha, oblivious to his plight, continued, "It would be the perfect solution to body odor in hot climates. And think of the branding! I'd market it as Dhoop Darling or Marine Drive Mist."

"And you think I'm the impractical one," Indro said, adjusting the collar of his plaid shirt. His relationship with plaid was a recent development, thanks to hours spent doomscrolling Derek Guy's sartorial pronouncements on Twitter. "Do you know what Derek says about hot-weather fabrics?"

"Does Derek live in Mumbai?" Tasha asked, her tone dripping with skepticism.

"No," Indro admitted. "But he's a fabric whisperer. Says plaid is a bold choice, perfect for casual refinement." "Bold choice?" Tasha scoffed, eyeing Indro's plaid shirt with the kind of disdain usually reserved for soggy biscuits. "You're sweating like a samosa in a steam bath. If Derek saw you right now, he'd disown you."

Indro tugged at his collar, his glower as dignified as a man wilting in the Mumbai heat could muster. "Tweed would have been worse."

"Yes," Tasha agreed, with the tone of a seasoned critic sharpening her quill. "But only marginally. You'd have gone from looking like a sweaty picnic blanket to a well-dressed roast chicken."

Before Indro could deliver a rebuttal worthy of the ages—or at least of his mood—a streak of neon and velocity zipped past them. The blur resolved itself into a young woman on rollerblades, weaving through the throng with the precision of a tailor threading a needle. She skidded to a halt in front of a jewelry stall, her ponytail swishing like an exclamation point punctuating her entrance.

"That's Rhea," Indro said, nodding toward the newcomer.

"Rhea?" Tasha asked, watching the girl lean casually against the stall, as if rollerblading through chaos were the most natural thing in the world. "She doesn't look like someone who strolls through life."

"She doesn't stroll," Indro replied. "She rolls. Colleague of mine. Absolute marvel when it comes to efficiency—and occasionally, diplomacy. Although mostly, she just gets things done."

The jewelry vendor, evidently accustomed to her grand entrances, produced a velvet tray with the resigned enthusiasm of a man who knew exactly how this would play out. "Crescent moon pendant," he announced. "Silver. Eight hundred rupees. No bargaining."

"Done," Rhea said briskly, producing a folded bundle of notes from a pouch strapped to her rollerblade. "That's why I like you. No drama."

"Efficient," Tasha murmured approvingly.

"And direct," Indro added. "She once negotiated an office renovation budget during a coffee break."

Having completed her transaction, Rhea turned and spotted Indro. Her face lit up with the unmistakable delight of someone who had just found their favorite target for witty repartee. "Indro! What brings you to the Causeway? Don't tell me you're shopping for more plaid."

"Very funny," Indro said dryly. "Rhea, meet Tasha. She's my... friend, apparently."

"Apparently?" Tasha echoed, raising an eyebrow.

"It's a complex relationship," Indro said. "Involving a lot of unsolicited advice."

"Ah," Rhea said, extending a hand to Tasha. "Rhea. Skater, negotiator, and occasionally the person who stops Indro from making poor life choices."

"That sounds like a full-time job," Tasha said, shaking her hand.

"You have no idea," Rhea replied. "Anyway, I'd love to stay and chat, but I'm on a mission."

"Oh?" Tasha asked. "What kind of mission?"

"The kind that involves indigo jute bags and the Kala Ghoda Festival," Rhea said, already wheeling toward a nearby stall. "Come on, I'll explain."

They followed her to the indigo stall, where the vendor—a man with sharp eyes and an air of quiet dignity—was arranging bags with the precision of a jeweler. Upon seeing Rhea, he brightened. "Rhea! You're late."

"Traffic," Rhea said breezily. "Now, show me what's new."

The vendor held up a bag adorned with swirling blue patterns. "This one's called Mumbai Monsoon. Inspired by the rains."

"Perfect," Rhea said, inspecting the bag. "I'll take fifty."

"Fifty?" the vendor asked, blinking. "Are you hosting a conference?"

"No," Rhea said. "They're going to Kala Ghoda. My friend's NGO stall needs something authentic, and your bags are exactly that."

Tasha's eyes lit up. "That's brilliant. The festival is a great platform for artists and craftsmen."

"It is," Rhea agreed. "It's one of the few places where hawkers and small artisans get a chance to be seen. People always think of hawkers as a nuisance, but they're the soul of this city. Festivals like Kala Ghoda remind everyone of that."

"Well said," Tasha said. "But does it work? Do hawkers actually get representation there?"

"Not as much as they should," Rhea admitted. "The festival's organizers try, but the demand for big names and flashy stalls makes it hard for street vendors to compete. That's why NGO stalls help—they give people like Shinde here a way in."

The vendor, now packing the bags, looked up. "It's true. Without people like Rhea, I'd never get my bags to a place like Kala Ghoda."

"And if they don't sell?" Indro asked skeptically.

"They'll sell," Rhea said, tightening the straps on her rollerblade pouch. "And if they don't, I'll skate around the festival shouting about their craftsmanship until they do."

"Which will either make you a hero or get you escorted out," Indro said.

"Both are good stories," Rhea replied with a grin.

As the vendor handed her the packed bags, Rhea gave him a thumbs-up. "Don't worry, Shinde. By the end of the day, these bags will be the talk of Kala Ghoda."

"They'd better be," Shinde said. "Or I'll name a bag after you and charge double for it."

"Call it Momentum Madness," Tasha suggested.

"Or Controlled Chaos," Indro added.

With a jaunty wave, Rhea skated off, leaving behind a trail of determination and just a hint of neon. Tasha watched her disappear into the crowd, shaking her head in admiration.

"She's remarkable," Tasha said.

"She's unstoppable," Indro corrected. "And if she pulls this off, she'll have single-handedly improved Mumbai's civic representation of hawkers—on rollerblades."

The cacophony of Colaba Causeway was in full swing, a symphony of commerce conducted in multiple languages. Vendors switched from Hindi to Spanish to French with the ease of seasoned polyglots, pitching their wares to a global audience. One leather vendor, with the charisma of a Shakespearean actor, was loudly proclaiming to a group of sun-hatted tourists, "Señorita! Muy auténtico! Bollywood stars carry wallets like this!" Nearby, another was selling wooden elephants, calling out in French, "Madame, très chic, very rare!"

Indro paused, momentarily captivated by the linguistic gymnastics on display. "Tasha," he said, nodding toward a particularly animated scarf vendor. "This man could sell sand to a camel. Look at him—he's pitching scarves as though they're enchanted relics from a Bollywood epic."

Tasha, barely glancing up from a particularly vivid display of scarves, replied, "You'd do well to take notes. Maybe then you'd sell your ideas to our boss with half as much flair."

Before Indro could retort, his eye caught the shimmer of a scarf at a nearby stall. It was adorned with delicate peacock feather patterns, and he immediately thought of Tasha, who adored scarves as much as she pretended not to. Indro, ever the opportunist when it came to sneaky gestures, decided to make his move. "Wait here," he muttered, handing her bag back to her and darting toward the stall.

The scarf vendor, who had clearly spotted an easy mark, greeted Indro with a winning smile. "Ah, sir! This scarf—pure silk, hand-dyed, Bollywood-inspired. For you, only 2,000 rupees."

Indro raised an eyebrow. "Two thousand? Seems a bit steep."

The vendor leaned in, adopting a conspiratorial tone. "For tourists, sir, usually 3,500. But for you, a local—discounted."

"Discounted, eh?" Indro replied, his skepticism barely concealed. "And how much would a tourist pay if they spoke Hindi?"

The vendor chuckled, sensing Indro's point. "Tourists, sir—they don't know local prices. They pay more because, for them, it's about the experience. Locals—well, you know better."

Indro folded his arms. "So, locals get ignored, and tourists overpay. Seems fair."

The vendor shrugged, his smile waning slightly. "It's economics, sir. The rent here is high, and tourists are willing to pay. If I charged everyone fairly, I wouldn't cover my costs. Locals, they bargain hard—they understand the value."

As Indro haggled the scarf down to 1,200 rupees, he glanced back toward Tasha, who was now watching an unfolding scene with Mrs. Alvares at another stall. He thanked the vendor, tucked the scarf into his bag, and rejoined her just as Mrs. Alvares was finishing her negotiations.

"Three thousand five hundred rupees?" Mrs. Alvares was saying with a smile that suggested both amusement and exasperation. "For this scarf? My dear man, it's polyester pretending to be silk. I'll give you two hundred."

"Madam!" the vendor exclaimed, clutching the scarf as though it were the crown jewels. "This is premium quality! Bollywood stars wear scarves like this."

Mrs. Alvares leaned lightly on her cane. "Oh, I'm sure they do—after paying half the price at a discount sale. Two hundred. Not a paisa more."

The crowd of tourists, now thoroughly enthralled, edged closer. One whispered something in French to her companion, who began flipping through a guidebook as though searching for instructions on how to handle haggling virtuosos.

The vendor sighed theatrically. "Madam, you wound me. This is art."

"And this," Mrs. Alvares replied, gesturing to her cane, "is a walking stick. Shall we continue pointing out the obvious?"

A ripple of laughter spread through the gathering. After a few more minutes of good-natured back-and-forth, the vendor relented. "Two hundred it is."

As Mrs. Alvares handed over the money, she turned to the tourists with a gracious smile. "Always start in Hindi," she advised. "It shows respect—and makes the price come down faster."

Tasha, watching with admiration, leaned toward Indro. "She's incredible."

"She's efficient," Indro agreed. "But you heard the vendor earlier. They rely on tourists paying extra to keep afloat. Locals like Mrs. Alvares can haggle because they know the real value. Tourists? They're buying the story."

"Maybe that's the problem," Tasha said, thoughtful. "If these vendors had a better platform—festivals, for instance—they wouldn't have to overcharge tourists or rely on locals fighting for a fair price."

Indro nodded. "You're thinking Kala Ghoda?"

"Exactly," Tasha said. "It's the perfect solution. Vendors can showcase their work at fair prices, tell their stories directly, and attract both locals and tourists without the pressure of rent."

"Not bad," Indro said, smirking. "Big ideas for someone who just criticized my shirt."

"Your shirt deserves it," Tasha replied with a grin. "But the vendors here? They deserve better."

As Mrs. Alvares disappeared into the crowd, her new scarf swinging jauntily from her arm, Indro handed Tasha the peacock scarf. "Speaking of deserving better," he said casually, "this is for you."

Tasha's expression softened as she took the scarf. "Indro, you sneak. You're not terrible, you know."

"Don't tell anyone," Indro said, grinning as they merged back into the bustling crowd, the medley of voices and colours swirling around them like the heartbeat of Colaba itself.

The wallet vendor caught Indro's eye with a deft flick of his wrist, holding up a leather wallet embossed with swirling patterns that looked like something Aladdin might pull out for spare change. "Saheb," he called out in Marathi, "yachya peeth kavita lihita yetil! Ekdam perfect. Tumcha khissa changla disel!" (Sir, you could write poetry on this! Perfect for your pocket!)

Indro stopped mid-step, momentarily thrown by the poetic enthusiasm. "He's selling me a wallet and promising literary inspiration. How do you say no to that?"

Tasha stifled a laugh. "You don't, apparently. Let's see it."

The vendor took this as an invitation, stepping forward with the energy of a man who had perfected his art. "Bagha, saheb! Ha wallet khara chamatkar aahe. Bollywood star log yanna gheun jatat." (Look, sir! This wallet is a true marvel. Even Bollywood stars buy these!)

Indro tilted his head, examining the wallet. "Bollywood stars, you say? Do they also haggle, or is that privilege reserved for me?"

The vendor chuckled, switching seamlessly to Hindi. "Sir, Bollywood stars don't haggle. They just pay. But for you, only 2,500 rupees. A steal."

"Only 2,500?" Indro echoed; eyebrows raised. "Stealing might be the right word."

Tasha, now fully engaged, stepped closer to the stall. "These are beautiful," she admitted, running her fingers over the intricate designs. "But the marketing, Indro—the marketing's all wrong. He should be selling these online with stories about where they're made, who makes them. These could sell for ten times as much with the right branding."

The vendor, overhearing this, perked up. "Madam, you think so? But writing and marketing—where would we learn this? We only know how to make."

"That's the problem," Tasha said, turning to Indro. "It's not just a lack of opportunity; it's a lack of access to skills like social media or storytelling. Imagine if they could barter their craft for marketing help."

"Barter?" The vendor's ears visibly pricked up. "Madam, we barter often—goods for goods. Wallets for raw material. But for marketing?" He gestured at her wrists. "Like your bracelets—did you make them?"

Tasha glanced at her wrist, where vibrant braided threads wrapped snugly. "These? Yes, just embroidery threads. Why?"

"Teach me," the vendor said eagerly. "If we add these to our wallets, maybe they'll look even more beautiful. My sister and I—we can make them together."

"Deal," Tasha said with a grin, reaching into her bag. She pulled out a small bundle of threads and crouched beside the stall, weaving and knotting with the grace of a seasoned artisan. The vendor watched intently, mimicking her movements with surprising dexterity.

A small crowd gathered, intrigued by the impromptu workshop. Indro stood back, arms crossed, observing with quiet admiration. "You know," he said, "you could start a business just teaching hawkers these things. Thread techniques, marketing strategies—you'd be Mumbai's barter queen."

"Don't tempt me," Tasha replied, tying off the braid with a flourish. She handed the sample to the vendor, who clapped his hands in delight.

"Madam, this is fantastic! Here—take this wallet," he said, pressing a beautifully embossed piece into her hands. "Barter is fair, no?"

Tasha accepted it with a smile. "Fair enough. But remember—bartering skills can go further than bartering goods. Trade with someone who can help you market these online."

The vendor nodded thoughtfully. "Maybe one day, madam. For now, I'll practice the braiding."

Indro, ever the advocate of hydration, unscrewed the cap of his luminous green protein shaker with the air of a man about to accomplish something monumental. Tasha, catching sight of it, gave him a look that suggested she was reconsidering her entire friendship with him.

"Chocolate protein shake? Here? Among handcrafted wallets and street artistry?" she asked, her voice brimming with incredulity.

Indro, unfazed, tipped the shaker back for a sip. "I need fuel, Tasha. You don't just shop in Colaba—you survive it. And as I'm the only one here who's had the foresight to think of nutrition, I feel it's my duty to lead by example."

"Oh, you're leading, all right," Tasha muttered. "Straight to disaster."

Indro ignored her, savouring his shake with the satisfaction of a man whose foresight was about to be proved tragically inadequate. For at that very moment, the delivery cart, which had been precariously manoeuvring through the market, nudged a fruit cart with the gentle insistence of inevitability. The nudge was enough to send oranges tumbling in all directions, triggering a ripple effect that ricocheted through the narrow lane.

A tourist dodged an orange and stumbled into a selfie-taker, who in turn staggered backward, clipping Indro's arm mid-swig. What followed was less a spill and more a spectacular explosion. The protein shake, with all the enthusiasm of a caffeinated acrobat, launched itself from the shaker and landed squarely on Indro's chest, turning his plaid shirt into a chocolate-splattered masterpiece.

Tasha turned just in time to witness the aftermath and promptly burst into laughter. "Oh no," she gasped, clutching her sides. "Your poor protein shake!"

"My shake?" Indro sputtered, looking down at himself in horror. "What about my shirt? It's a crime scene!"

Before Tasha could respond, the wallet vendor materialized at Indro's side, holding out a neatly embroidered handkerchief with the gravitas of a knight offering a sword. "Here, madam," he said, addressing Tasha. "For your friend. A small gift to help."

Tasha, still stifling laughter, took the handkerchief. "Thank you," she said, reaching into her bag to pay for it. "How much?"

"Oh, madam, it's free," the vendor said magnanimously. "No one should walk around like this. It's bad for business."

"Nonsense," Tasha replied, handing him a crisp note. "This is worth every rupee just for the memory."

Indro dabbed at his shirt with the handkerchief, only managing to smear the chocolate into a pattern that now resembled a Rorschach test. "This," he declared solemnly, "is why I don't trust food outside a controlled environment."

Tasha grinned, tucking the wallet she'd just purchased into her bag. "Cheer up, Indro. You've just become a walking example of why people should stick to bottled water in markets. Very educational."

"And deeply humiliating," Indro muttered, glaring at the offending shaker as though it had betrayed him on purpose. "From now on, I'm sticking to samosas. They'd cost you less than.. hey, what did you pay for the kerchief?"

"Tourist rates, Tasha quipped, as the wallet vendor gave Indro a consoling pat on the back and returned to his stall.

As the oranges were finally rounded up and the street settled back into its usual hum, Indro sighed. "I'd say this market is unforgiving."

"No," Tasha replied, her grin widening. "It's unforgettable. Just like you, chocolate blotches and all."

As they walked away, Nugget found them again trotting after them briefly before deciding the scarves were a better throne. Tasha sighed. "This place is beautiful, but it's so broken."

"Maybe it's not broken," Indro said. "It's just… Mumbai."

"And Nugget?"

"He's the king," Indro said. "And he knows it."

Chapter 7

Mastery in Motion of the Incredible Local

Mumbai's mornings begin with a rush that doesn't ask for permission. Dadar Station, an unrelenting vortex of commuters and cacophony, was in full swing. The platforms pulsed with life: hawkers shouting their wares, announcements blaring in three languages, and the rhythmic roar of trains arriving and departing like clockwork—or something close to it.

Tasha strode confidently, her scarf fluttering behind her, as Indro trailed behind, clutching his bag as if it might grow legs and escape.

"All right, rookie," Tasha said, smirking as she eyed him. "Men's compartments are over there. We're meeting at Churchgate. Stick to the plan, and you'll survive."

"And if I don't?" Indro asked, scanning the crowd with growing alarm.

"Then you'll get a scenic tour of Virar," she said with a shrug. "Call me if you get lost. And for heaven's sake, don't try standing at the door like one of those door-danglers. You're not auditioning for a Bollywood remake."

The train screeched into the station, its brakes singing the symphony of a long day ahead. Before Indro could gather his thoughts, the tide of humanity swallowed him, shoving him into the men's compartment. Tasha disappeared into the ladies' section with practiced grace, her laughter carried away by the din.

The train roared into the station; its approach announced by a screech that sounded like it might have come from a prehistoric creature rather than a piece of modern engineering. The platform, already a swirling vortex of humanity, transformed into a full-blown stampede.

"Stick close!" Tasha yelled, her voice barely audible over the cacophony of metal on metal. "And for heaven's sake, keep moving!"

Indro's reply was lost in the din, but his face—a fascinating study in dread—spoke volumes. The train hadn't even stopped, yet people were already attempting to board, flinging themselves at the open doorways as though the train might disappear into thin air if they didn't claim their place. The fact that the train had no doors to shut out the madness only seemed to encourage this daring assault.

"Why aren't they waiting?" Indro shouted, dodging an umbrella-wielding auntie whose strategy for entry involved brute force and a sharp elbow.

"Waiting?" Tasha called back with a grin. "That's a luxury only the rich and the foolish can afford in Mumbai."

She slipped into the melee with practiced ease, her movements as fluid as water finding its way through a narrow crack. Indro, meanwhile, found himself caught between a man balancing a teetering tower of tiffins and a student clutching a backpack large enough to house a small family.

Inside the train, alighting passengers were valiantly attempting to exit, but they were no match for the flood of bodies pouring in. There were shouts of "Arre bhai, let us get down first!"—requests that were ignored with the enthusiasm of New Year's resolutions forgotten by February.

Indro watched in horror as the crowd surged forward again, sweeping him toward the train like a leaf caught in a monsoon current. He stumbled through the doorless opening, propelled not by choice but by the collective momentum of fifty impatient commuters behind him. His entry was less "step aboard" and more "land like a sack of potatoes."

"Mind your feet!" a voice barked as Indro barely missed stepping on someone's shoe. He found himself inside, miraculously upright, with the train already rumbling into motion. He glanced back at the open doorway, where a young man perched on the edge of the floor, one hand casually gripping the frame, the other holding a phone as though taking a call while dangling out of a speeding train was the most natural thing in the world.

"Are there no doors on these trains?" Indro asked the man nearest him, his voice a mix of incredulity and despair.

"Doors?" The man laughed heartily, his head tipping back. "Who has time for doors? This is Mumbai, boss. We're too busy getting in and out!"

Indro made a mental note to write a will at the earliest opportunity.

Indro's first lesson in Mumbai's train culture came as a rude awakening—literally. A man's elbow jabbed his ribs as the train lurched forward, and Indro clutched the nearest pole like a shipwreck survivor clinging to driftwood. Around him, the men's compartment thrummed with energy. Conversations layered over the metallic clatter of the train, creating a soundscape uniquely Mumbai.

The air was heavy with the mingling scents of sweat, deodorant bravely fighting a losing battle, and the faint tang of oil from someone's breakfast pakora. Indro winced as a sharp jolt sent him careening into the tiffin-carrying man he had seen earlier.

"Steady, steady!" the man said with a good-natured grin. "You have to find your balance, or the train will teach you its own way."

"I'm trying," Indro muttered, adjusting his glasses and planting his feet wider apart. "But this feels more like surviving than traveling."

The man laughed. "That's the spirit! I'm Akshay, by the way. Eight years on these tracks. And you?"

"Indro," he replied, still gripping the pole as though his life depended on it. "First day. I feel like I'm failing an exam I didn't even study for."

Akshay chuckled. "You'll pass. Everyone does, eventually. Just avoid standing near the door unless you want to lose a toe. Or worse, your dignity."

Indro nodded, glancing around at the other men in the compartment. A few clutched their phones, some read newspapers, and one man was fast asleep, his head lolling precariously with every sway of the train. What struck Indro most, however, was the attire—or lack thereof.

"Is there... a dress code for this train?" Indro asked cautiously, nodding toward a man in a pair of shorts so short they seemed to defy reason.

Akshay followed his gaze and grinned. "Ah, you've noticed. Men's fashion here isn't dictated by style—it's dictated by survival. See that guy in the shorts? He's dressed for ventilation, not aesthetics."

"And the one with the tie?" Indro asked, eyeing another commuter whose crisply ironed shirt and tie seemed completely out of place in the chaos.

"That's Mr. Corporate," Akshay said, lowering his voice conspiratorially. "He probably dressed like that in the hopes of getting a seat. People are less likely to shove a guy in a tie, or so he thinks. It's a tactic."

Indro raised an eyebrow. "Does it work?"

"Not a chance," Akshay replied, laughing. "But hope is a powerful thing."

As the train screeched to a halt at the next station, the crowd shifted like a tidal wave, commuters jostling for position. Indro noticed a group of men jumping off the train before it had fully stopped, darting toward the platform's edge.

"Are they... running?" Indro asked, bewildered.

"Trying to avoid the queues at the ticket counter," Akshay explained. "Not everyone has the app or enough balance on their travel cards. And have you seen the lines? They look like they belong at a ration shop in 1947."

"Can't they just... wait their turn?" Indro ventured.

Akshay snorted. "You're new here, aren't you? Waiting is a luxury Mumbai doesn't have. Time is everything. You waste it, you lose it."

Indro frowned. "It's so... frantic. Doesn't anyone slow down?"

"Not unless they want to get left behind," Akshay said with a shrug. "But it's not just about speed. Men have their own struggles in this city. Finding a clean public restroom, for one. You'd think a place that moves this fast would have better facilities."

Indro's stomach tightened as he recalled his earlier panic about restrooms. "You don't say."

"And then there's the battle for personal space," Akshay continued. "You're standing here now, but wait until the evening rush. You won't just be touching shoulders—you'll be touching souls."

Indro gave him a skeptical look. "You're exaggerating."

"Am I?" Akshay replied with a wicked grin. "Just wait. By the end of the day, you'll know the brands of deodorant half the compartment uses. Or doesn't use."

As the train approached the next station, the crowd shifted again, and Indro found himself pressed against the door.

Akshay reached out to steady him, chuckling. "Relax. The city will knock you around a bit, but it won't let you fall—at least not often."

Indro attempted a smile. "And here I thought my biggest worry would be missing my stop."

Akshay's expression softened. "You'll get the hang of it. Mumbai trains aren't just transportation—they're a way of life. Once you learn the rhythm, it's like dancing. A chaotic, sweaty, slightly smelly dance."

Indro laughed despite himself. "I'm not sure I'm ready for that yet."

"You will be," Akshay said, slapping his shoulder. "By the time this train reaches Churchgate, you'll be a different man."

As the train lurched forward again, Indro glanced out at the passing cityscape, a mix of dilapidated buildings and gleaming skyscrapers. Despite the chaos, there was something intoxicating about the relentless motion. He wasn't ready to admit it yet, but Akshay was probably right.

Indro clung to the pole, and his confidence in survival began to grow. Perhaps Akshay's advice had some merit after all. He glanced at the satchel slung over his shoulder, where his trusty protein shake awaited. A moment of replenishment seemed in order.

Carefully, he unscrewed the cap of his shaker, a fluorescent green vessel that could rival any Mumbai autorickshaw for sheer gaudiness. The chocolate aroma wafted up, bringing him a sense of calm amidst the chaos.

Akshay glanced at the shaker and grinned. "Protein shake on a Mumbai local? Bold move."

"It's a necessity," Indro replied. "This is my lifeline."

"You might want to rethink that," Akshay said, just as the train screeched to a halt at the next station.

The sudden jolt sent the compartment into an uncoordinated sway. Indro, mid-sip, felt the contents of his shaker take on a life of their own. With the force of a geyser, the chocolate shake erupted, splattering his shirt, glasses, and, most unforgivably, the tie-wearing commuter beside him.

The tie-wearer stared at Indro, his expression one of stunned horror. "What is this? A dessert buffet?"

"I—uh—" Indro stammered, clutching the now half-empty shaker. "It's protein. Chocolate flavour."

"Chocolate flavour? On my tie?" the man exclaimed, attempting to wipe the stain with a handkerchief that only made matters worse.

Akshay, clearly enjoying the spectacle, handed Indro his own handkerchief with a grin. "First rule of Mumbai trains: Don't tempt fate with open liquids."

Indro dabbed at his shirt, muttering, "This city has a vendetta against me."

As the train approached the next station, the compartment erupted into its usual shuffle, leaving Indro both sticky and chastened. Akshay patted him on the back. "Cheer up. You'll fit right in once you stop trying to fight the rhythm."

"And stop drinking protein shakes on the move," added the tie-wearer darkly, glaring at the chocolate blotch that now adorned his otherwise pristine attire.

As the ladies' compartment jolted into motion, Tasha adjusted her scarf with the practiced ease of someone who knew every sway, bump, and lurch of Mumbai's local trains. She glanced at the woman sitting across from her—a trim figure in a perfectly pressed kurta, her hair styled into a sharp bob. The woman was scribbling furiously in a notebook, her pen racing against the train's rhythm.

"Are you planning to redesign the city?" Tasha asked with a smile, breaking the silence.

The woman looked up, startled for a moment, before returning the smile. "Not yet. But if I did, I'd start with this train."

"Good luck with that," Tasha said, laughing. "I was born in Bombay, and the trains haven't changed a bit. Same bumps, same smells, same chaos. It's oddly comforting."

"Bombay, is it?" the woman asked, arching an eyebrow. "Not Mumbai?"

"Always Bombay," Tasha replied with mock solemnity. "Mumbai feels like it's wearing someone else's clothes. Bombay is what it was meant to be."

The woman chuckled. "Interesting. You're clinging to the past, then?"

"Not clinging," Tasha said, tilting her head thoughtfully. "Appreciating. Bombay had charm. Mumbai has determination.

It's the same city, but one feels like a friend, and the other... an overworked boss."

The woman nodded, setting her notebook aside. "Fair enough. I'm Maya, by the way—civil engineer, professional scribbler, and occasional train philosopher."

"Tasha," she replied, shaking Maya's outstretched hand. "Born in Bombay, dreaming in Mumbai."

Maya glanced out the window as the train pulled into a station, her eyes catching the faded lettering of an old sign partially painted over. "Look at that," she said, gesturing to it. "The past always peeks through, no matter how much we try to erase it."

Tasha followed her gaze. "That's the problem with renaming things. It's never just about the name—it's about power. Who has the right to decide what a place should be called?"

Maya nodded thoughtfully. "And who gets to remember what it was called? Renaming is supposed to honor something—a person, a culture, a cause—but it often feels like a way of burying what came before. It's not about honouring the new; it's about erasing the old."

"It's elitist," Tasha said, her voice sharpening. "You can't just rename a place and expect the people who live there to adapt overnight. Names carry memory, habit, identity. When you change them, you create confusion—not progress."

Maya smiled wryly. "But isn't that the point? Confusion keeps people focused on the present, on survival. It's hard to fight for the past when you're just trying to get through your day."

Tasha leaned forward. "Exactly. It's like renaming stations. Sure, you can call it Prabhadevi to honor a goddess, but to the millions of commuters rushing through it, it's Lower Parel. That's the name they grew up with, the name that carries their stories."

Maya tilted her head. "But don't you think there's a beauty in letting the old and the new coexist? In Mumbai, the two are always intertwined—every renamed station is still its old self, just hidden under a new layer."

"Maybe," Tasha said. "But it feels like painting over a masterpiece with something less inspired. The old names had a rhythm, a charm. Victoria Terminus. Churchgate. Even Bombay. You change them, and it's like giving the city a haircut it didn't ask for."

Maya laughed. "The city doesn't care what you call it, Tasha. It just keeps moving."

Tasha smiled. "Maybe. But the people care. And that's what makes the city what it is."

In the swaying ladies' compartment, conversations hummed along a familiar rhythm—snippets of gossip, whispered prayers, the occasional barked instruction to a child clinging to their mother's sari. Tasha leaned back in her seat, letting the warm cadence of life wash over her, when a sharp voice cut through the hum.

"You can't just leave your bag on the seat and expect it to stay yours!"

The voice belonged to a woman in her late 40s, her face framed by the loose end of her dupatta. Her tone was clipped, almost rehearsed, as though she had delivered this particular argument many times before.

"And you can't just grab it when it's clearly marked," retorted a younger woman, clutching the edge of the disputed seat as though it were a lifeline. Her hair was frizzed by the humidity, and her eyes carried the strain of a long day.

"It's a train, not your private car!" snapped the older woman. "You think I have time to hold my bag in my lap all the way from Kalyan?"

The compartment's air thickened, tension curling into every corner. The other passengers turned toward the spat with the detached interest of people who knew better than to intervene.

"Why don't you both sit down?" suggested a grandmotherly figure across the aisle, her voice kind but weary. "You're squabbling over a seat when there's room for two backsides if you just shuffle a bit."

The younger woman glared. "It's not about the space. It's about respect."

Tasha tilted her head slightly, intrigued. There was something about the sharpness in the younger woman's voice that spoke of more than just frustration over seating. This wasn't just about a seat—it was a contest of dignity, a small skirmish in a larger, unspoken war.

The older woman huffed, tugging her bag off the seat as though conceding the argument out of pity rather than defeat. "Respect?" she echoed bitterly. "We're all trying to survive, madam. Respect doesn't get you a seat. It gets you nothing."

Her words hung in the air, weighty and familiar. Around her, a few women nodded quietly, their eyes flickering with recognition.

The younger woman hesitated, the steel in her posture softening. "It's just..." she began, before faltering. "It's not fair. We spend the whole day... out there." She gestured vaguely toward the world outside the train, where deadlines, catcalls, and expectations awaited. "And then we come in here, and it's the same thing. You must fight for every inch, every breath."

"It's not just here," the older woman said, her tone softening. "It's everywhere. Seats, salaries, sidewalks—it's all the same. You think I don't know?"

For a moment, the compartment grew quiet, the clatter of the train filling the space where their voices had been. The grandmotherly figure across the aisle sighed deeply, her eyes trained on the window. "You know," she said, "I've been taking this train for forty years, and I've seen fights like this every day. Not much has changed. But at least here, we're all in it together."

The words seemed to settle the air. The younger woman nodded, finally releasing her grip on the seat. She slid into it alongside the older woman, their elbows brushing but no longer hostile.

Tasha smiled faintly to herself, her gaze drifting back out the window. Mumbai's trains weren't just transportation; they were theatres of survival, their compartments a stage for the dramas of everyday life. Fights over seats weren't just about seats. They were about the bruises women carried from the outside world, the unrelenting need to carve out a place for themselves, even if it was just eighteen inches of metal in a crowded train.

The train jolted slightly, and Tasha leaned back, letting the rhythm of the city take over again. As the women resumed their silence, the compartment felt less like a battlefield and more like a shared truce—however temporary it might be.

As the train rattled along, Indro's internal discomfort grew more insistent - a pressing reminder of the perils of overindulgence in morning tea. He leaned toward a fellow passenger, a middle-aged man engrossed in a newspaper.

"Excuse me," Indro began, attempting to sound casual despite the urgency knotting his insides. "Could you tell me where the nearest restroom is?"

The man lowered his paper, eyeing Indro with a mix of sympathy and amusement. "Restroom? On this train?" He chuckled, shaking his head. "You're new here, aren't you?"

Indro managed a tight-lipped smile. "Is it that obvious?"

"Only to those who've danced this dance before," the man replied. "Your best bet is to get off at the next station and find facilities there. But be quick about it—trains wait for no one."

"Thank you," Indro said, though his gratitude was laced with anxiety. He glanced at the route map plastered above the windows, trying to decipher the maze of lines and dots. The names blurred together, each more foreign than the last.

The train's speakers crackled to life, emitting a garbled announcement that did little to clarify matters. Indro caught fragments—something about the next station—but the rest was swallowed by static and the ambient clamour of the compartment.

He turned to another passenger, a young man tapping away on his phone. "Pardon me, which station is next?"

The young man didn't look up. "Prabhadevi," he muttered, more focused on his screen than the conversation.

Indro nodded, though the name meant nothing to him. He fished out his own phone, hoping to consult a map or app for guidance. But, as luck would have it, the screen remained stubbornly blank—no signal in this metal tube hurtling through the city.

The train began to slow, and Indro braced himself. As the doors slid open, he joined the throng spilling onto the platform. He scanned the area for signs, but the crush of bodies and the labyrinthine layout made navigation a challenge.

Spotting a station attendant, Indro hurried over. "Excuse me, could you point me to the restroom?"

The attendant barely glanced up. "Down the platform, to the left," he said, waving a hand in a vague direction.

Indro followed the gesture, weaving through the crowd. He found the facilities—a modest structure with a modest queue. Joining the line, he tapped his foot impatiently, the seconds ticking away in his mind.

Finally, his turn came. He hurried through his business, emerging with a sense of relief that was short-lived. The unmistakable sound of a departing train reached his ears.

He dashed back to the platform, only to see the train he'd arrived on pulling away.

"Wonderful," he muttered, scanning the timetable for the next arrival. The schedule was a cryptic puzzle, and without a reliable app or clear announcements, he felt adrift.

As he navigated the bustling platform, he fumbled for his phone and dialed Tasha's number.

"Tasha," he began, trying to mask his urgency, "I've had to get off the train. Which station am I at?"

"Can you see a sign?" Tasha's voice crackled through the line.

Indro squinted at the nearest signboard. "It says 'Prabhadevi.'"

"Just board the next southbound train from Elphinstone," Tasha instructed. "It'll take you straight to Churchgate."

"Southbound," Indro repeated, scanning the platform for any indication of direction. "And how do I know which train is southbound?"

"Look for the indicators," Tasha suggested. "Or follow the crowd; most people here are headed south in the morning."

As Indro tried to make sense of the station's signage, the line crackled, and Tasha's voice became faint. "Tasha? Tasha, are you there?" The call dropped, leaving Indro with a half-formed plan and a platform teeming with commuters.

He glanced around, hoping for a map or a helpful announcement, but the station offered no such luxuries. The public address system emitted only static, and the electronic boards displayed a cryptic array of numbers and destinations.

Amidst this orchestrated chaos, a voice cut through the din. "You look like a man in need of a map," it observed with a chuckle.

Indro turned to find a gentleman of indeterminate age, his attire a curious blend of colonial-era elegance and modern-day practicality. The man's eyes twinkled with the kind of mischief that suggested he found the world perpetually amusing.

"Sudhir," the man introduced himself, extending a hand.

"Indro," he replied, shaking the offered hand. "And you wouldn't be wrong. This station—Prabhadevi, is it?—has me thoroughly perplexed."

"Ah, the artist formerly known as Elphinstone Road," Sudhir said with a grin. "The station was renamed in July 2018 to honor the local deity Prabhadevi and to shed its colonial-era name. And depending on whom you ask, it might still be Lower Parel, although that's another station. Mumbai has a penchant for rechristening its landmarks, leaving us mere mortals to play catch-up."

Indro sighed, the weight of the city's capricious nomenclature adding to his fatigue. "I need to get to Churchgate. Tasha—my friend—mentioned boarding a southbound train, but the directions here are as clear as mud."

Sudhir nodded sympathetically. "The signage is a riddle, the announcements are a test of one's auditory prowess, and the apps... well, let's just say they're as reliable as the monsoon. But fret not; I shall be your Virgil through this inferno."

He led Indro toward the edge of the platform, where the crowd ebbed and flowed with a rhythm that defied logic. "Observe," Sudhir instructed. "The masses have an unspoken understanding of where to stand, when to move, and how to squeeze into spaces that would make a contortionist weep."

As they waited, Sudhir continued, his tone taking on a more serious note. "Navigating this city's transit system is an art form, one that requires patience, intuition, and a certain level of resignation. The lack of clear information, the overcrowding, the delays—it's a daily crucible that tests the mettle of even the most seasoned commuter."

Indro listened, absorbing the wisdom laced with humour. "And yet, people endure."

"Indeed," Sudhir agreed. "Because beneath the chaos lies a resilience that defines Mumbai. It's a city that demands much but offers much in return—if you know how to navigate its idiosyncrasies."

A train thundered into the station, its arrival heralded by a gust of wind and the collective shuffling of feet. Sudhir placed a steadying hand on Indro's shoulder. "Remember, my friend: in this city, hesitation is your enemy. Move with purpose, and the city will carry you along."

With that, they plunged into the fray, boarding the train that would, with any luck, deliver Indro to his destination—and perhaps, in time, to a deeper understanding of the city that had, in its own chaotic way, begun to embrace him.

As the next train approached, Sudhir leaned casually against a pillar, his eyes twinkling with the amusement of a man well-acquainted with the city's quirks. Indro stood beside him, still catching his breath, clutching his satchel as though it might spring to life and abscond at any moment.

"You're adapting swiftly," Sudhir remarked, nodding toward the satchel. "But remember, Mumbai is a city that thrives on surprises. Vigilance is your best companion."

Indro managed a weary nod, his nerves still jangling like loose change. His gaze wandered to a group entering the adjacent platform—an eclectic trio adorned in vibrant attire, moving with a confidence that parted the crowd like the Red Sea. They clapped their hands in a rhythmic, almost ceremonial manner as they navigated the throng, pausing occasionally to exchange words or gestures with passengers. Some commuters handed over small notes without a word; others fixed their eyes on distant, imaginary horizons.

Perplexed, Indro glanced at Sudhir. "Who are they?" he inquired hesitantly.

Following Indro's gaze, Sudhir's expression softened with understanding. "Ah," he began, "they are an integral part of this city's tapestry—have been for centuries. You'll encounter them on trains, at traffic signals, even at weddings. Some view their presence as a blessing; others, perhaps, as an intrusion. But in truth, they are neither."

Indro observed the trio's demeanour—heads held high, unapologetically present, their laughter rising above the station's din. "People seem... divided about them."

"They're not easily categorized," Sudhir mused. "And that's precisely why they've endured every transformation this city has undergone. Mumbai embraces everyone, even when it doesn't fully understand how."

Nearby, a woman handed over a crisp note, receiving a dramatic blessing in return. The exchange concluded with mutual smiles, leaving both parties seemingly lighter. "It's... unusual," Indro remarked, searching for the right words.

"It's Mumbai," Sudhir replied simply. "A mosaic of countless stories."

As they continued to wait, Sudhir's attention shifted to a group of men clad in white attire and distinctive caps, expertly manoeuvring through the throng with crates of lunchboxes. "Observe those gentlemen," he said, "The dabbawalas. They deliver over 130,000 lunches daily across Mumbai with remarkable precision. Their system is so efficient that a 2010 Harvard Business School study rated it at Six Sigma, meaning they make fewer than 3.4 errors per million transactions."

Indro watched in amazement as the dabbawalas navigated the crowded platform with practiced ease. "That's incredible," he remarked.

Sudhir nodded, then gestured toward an approaching train. "And here comes an AC EMU—Air-Conditioned Electrical Multiple Unit. Quieter, less crowded, but more expensive. It's a different experience from the regular compartments."

As the train doors slid open, a rush of cool air spilled onto the platform. Commuters stepped in, their expressions a mix of relief and indifference. Sudhir continued, "These trains are great if you want Mumbai without the madness. But where's the fun in that?"

Indro chuckled, appreciating Sudhir's perspective. "So, it's about choosing between comfort and the authentic experience?"

"Exactly," Sudhir replied. "But beyond the choice of trains, commuters face several challenges daily."

He pointed toward a group of individuals moving through the crowd, clapping rhythmically as they approached passengers. "For instance, interactions with them can be uncomfortable for some. They often seek alms, and while many see it as a cultural nuance, others find it intrusive."

Indro observed as some passengers handed over small notes, while others avoided eye contact. "It seems like a delicate balance," he noted.

"It is," Sudhir agreed. "Then there's the issue of overcrowding. Despite being the lifeline of the city, our trains are often packed beyond capacity, leading to safety concerns."

Indro recalled the sardine-like conditions he had experienced earlier. "I felt that firsthand," he admitted.

Sudhir sighed. "Yes, and it's not just about comfort. Overcrowding has led to accidents and fatalities. The Bombay High Court even criticized the railways for the alarming number of deaths, calling for urgent action."

Indro's eyes widened. "I had no idea it was that severe."

"Unfortunately, it is," Sudhir confirmed. "And while the introduction of AC locals was meant to provide relief, it hasn't been smooth. There have been protests against replacing non-AC locals with AC ones, as many commuters find the fares unaffordable."

Indro watched as a group of passengers argued with railway staff near an AC train. "It seems like a complex issue," he observed.

"Indeed," Sudhir said. "The railway system is a microcosm of the city's challenges—overpopulation, infrastructure strain, and socio-economic disparities."

As the next train approached, Sudhir turned to Indro with a wry smile. "Remember, Mumbai moves fast. Keep up, and you'll be fine."

Indro nodded, feeling a newfound respect for the city's commuters and the daily battles they faced.

With a final pat on Indro's shoulder, Sudhir melted into the crowd, leaving Indro to navigate the bustling platform with a deeper understanding of Mumbai's heartbeat.

Resigned to the whims of fate, Indro decided to follow the largest group of passengers, reasoning that the collective wisdom of the masses might lead him in the right direction. As he joined the throng edging toward the platform's edge, a train thundered in, its open doors revealing a densely packed interior.

With a deep breath and a silent prayer, Indro braced himself for another plunge into Mumbai's chaotic embrace, hoping that this time, it would deposit him at his intended destination.

The train screeched into Churchgate station, and Indro braced himself for the dismount. The crowd began to surge toward the door even before the train stopped, and he was swept along, his grip on his satchel faltering.

As the train jolted to a halt, he stumbled onto the platform, barely managing to regain his balance. The satchel, his lifeline through the chaos of the day, slipped from his hand and fell into the narrow gap between the platform and the train.

For a moment, he froze, panic coursing through him. The train was already whistling its intent to move on. Commuters darted around him, some shouting, others cursing his clumsiness.

"Bhai, move!" a man barked as he narrowly avoided colliding with Indro.

"My bag!" Indro exclaimed, pointing helplessly toward the tracks where the satchel lay, wedged in the gravel.

Suddenly, a pair of hands grabbed his shoulders and pulled him aside. "Stay out of the way!" a familiar voice commanded.

Indro turned to see Tasha, her face a mixture of irritation and concern. "You look like a lost puppy," she said. "What happened?"

"My bag—it's down there!" Indro pointed again, his voice rising. "It has my phone, my notes, everything!"

Tasha groaned but quickly sprang into action. "Stay here," she ordered, before waving at a station attendant.

"Excuse me! My friend dropped his bag on the tracks. Can you help?" she asked, her voice firm but polite.

The attendant glanced at the bag, then at the train, which was now creaking ominously as it prepared to leave. "You'll have to wait for the next train to pass," he said, already turning away.

"Next train?" Indro asked, his voice climbing. "That could be ages!"

Tasha rolled her eyes. "Not in Mumbai, genius. It'll be here in two minutes."

As they waited, a scruffy orange cat trotted across the platform, seemingly oblivious to the chaos around it. Nugget. The self-appointed king of Prabhadevi had somehow made his way to Churchgate, or perhaps another cat in the lineage of Mumbai's platform royalty was taking up the mantle.

Nugget hopped down onto the tracks with feline indifference, sniffed at Indro's bag, and gave it a lazy nudge with his paw.

"Is that... Nugget?" Indro asked, bewildered.

"It's a cat," Tasha said impatiently. "Focus!"

The attendant returned with a long stick, muttering something about "rookie mistakes" as he expertly hooked the satchel and hoisted it back onto the platform.

"There," he said, handing it over to Indro. "Next time, keep a better grip."

Indro clutched his bag, relief flooding his face. But as he opened it to check its contents, his expression darkened. "Where's my phone?" he asked, rummaging through the satchel.

"You had your phone in your hand when you called me," Tasha pointed out. "Don't tell me you—"

"Dropped it too," Indro finished, groaning. "It must still be on the train!"

Tasha sighed, pinching the bridge of her nose. "Okay, let's not panic. We'll call your number. Someone might pick up."

She took out her own phone and dialed his number. To Indro's astonishment, the call connected immediately.

"Hello?" came a voice from the other end, muffled by the background noise of the train.

"This is the owner of the phone," Indro said quickly. "Where are you?"

"I'm on my way to Virar," the voice replied. "But don't worry—I'll leave it with the lost-and-found at Andheri."

"Andheri?" Indro repeated, his voice breaking. "That's so far!"

Tasha couldn't suppress her laughter. "Welcome to Mumbai," she said, shaking her head. "You wanted drama. The city delivers."

Chapter 8

Mastery Under Monsoon Skies

The monsoon had unleashed its annual deluge upon Mumbai, transforming the city into a labyrinth of waterlogged streets and overflowing drains. In the upscale neighborhood of Juhu, nestled amidst swaying palm trees and colonial-era bungalows, stood "Sundar Niket," the erstwhile residence of Indro's uncle. The bungalow, with its whitewashed walls and terracotta-tiled roof, exuded an old-world charm. Its expansive garden, once a verdant sanctuary of hibiscus and frangipani, now resembled a miniature lake, with water lapping perilously close to the veranda steps.

Indro stood at the threshold, surveying the watery expanse with a mixture of dismay and determination. Clad in a rain-drenched kurta and rolled-up trousers, he wielded a plastic bucket, valiantly attempting to bail out the encroaching water. Each splash seemed a Sisyphean effort against the relentless monsoon.

As he emptied yet another bucket, the distant hum of an approaching scooter caught his attention. Moments later, Tasha arrived, her vibrant yellow raincoat contrasting starkly with the gray monotony of the overcast sky. Nugget, her ever-enthusiastic canine companion, trotted beside her, shaking off droplets with every step.

"Battling the elements, I see," Tasha remarked, her eyes twinkling with amusement.

Indro managed a wry smile. "Just trying to keep the ark afloat."

Tasha glanced around, taking in the submerged garden and the forlorn flowerbeds. "Have you tried calling for a pump?"

Indro nodded, a hint of frustration creeping into his voice. "I did. The housekeeper left a list of contacts for emergencies like this. But no one's answering. It's as if the entire city's on voicemail."

Tasha sighed, casting a sympathetic glance at the waterlogged garden. "Looks like we'll have to venture out and find one ourselves."

Indro agreed, and after securing the bungalow, the trio set off into the neighborhood. The rain had mercifully ceased, leaving behind a world washed clean yet fraught with challenges. Puddles reflected the somber sky, and the air was thick with the earthy aroma of petrichor.

As Tasha and Indro navigated the rain-soaked streets of Juhu, Tasha softly hummed the melancholic tune of

R.D. Burman's classic, "Tujhse nārāz nahīṅ zindagī, hairān hūṅ main..." The melody intertwined with the rhythmic patter of residual raindrops, creating a poignant symphony.

Indro, ever the intellectual, seized the moment to delve into meteorological musings. "You know, the monsoon's arrival is heralded by the formation of specific cloud types."

Tasha glanced at the sky, her brow furrowing slightly. "Cumulonimbus... those are the big, fluffy ones that look like cotton candy, right?" Tasha's curiosity about the towering clouds overhead prompted a discussion. "Indro, these massive clouds— How exactly do they form?"

"Ah, They begin as humble cumulus clouds, formed when the sun heats the Earth's surface, causing warm, moist air to rise—a process known as convection. As this air ascends, it cools, and the moisture condenses into water droplets, creating clouds. With sufficient atmospheric instability, these clouds can develop into towering cumulonimbus, reaching heights up to 12 kilometres or more."

"So, they're like the overachievers of the cloud world, starting small and aiming high?"

"Precisely, Indro affirmed, a hint of admiration in his voice. Their vertical development is impressive, often penetrating the upper troposphere. This extensive growth allows them to hold vast amounts of water, leading to heavy rainfall and thunderstorms."

"And during Mumbai's monsoon, these clouds are the main culprits behind our torrential downpours?"

"Indeed. The southwest monsoon brings moist air from the Arabian Sea, which, upon reaching the Western Ghats and the city, rises and cools, forming these formidable clouds. Their presence is synonymous with the intense rainfall characteristic of our monsoon season."

"Fascinating, Indro. So, next time I see these towering clouds, I'll know to carry an umbrella—and perhaps a boat."

"A wise precaution. Cumulonimbus clouds are not only harbingers of rain but can also bring thunderstorms and, occasionally, hail. Their grandeur is matched only by their unpredictability."

Tasha nodded, her fingers brushing against the rain-kissed leaves of a nearby gulmohar tree. "And what about the winds? They seem to have a mind of their own during the monsoon."

"Indeed," Indro replied, his tone taking on a lecturing cadence. "During the monsoon, Mumbai experiences prevailing southwesterly winds, a result of the southwest monsoon system. These winds transport moist air from the Arabian Sea, leading to the characteristic heavy rains of the season."

Tasha tilted her head, a playful smile tugging at her lips. "Southwest, northeast... I must confess, directions baffle me. If I'm facing one way, north is in front; if I turn around, it's behind me. How do you make sense of it all?"

Indro chuckled softly, appreciating her candidness. "Think of directions as fixed points on a map. North is always towards the North Pole, south towards the

South Pole, regardless of which way you're facing. If you're facing north, east is to your right and west to your left. Turn around to face south, and east is now to your left, west to your right. The directions themselves don't change; it's our orientation that shifts."

Tasha's eyes sparkled with newfound understanding. "Ah, so it's about aligning oneself with the cardinal points, independent of personal perspective."

"Exactly," Indro affirmed, his gaze lingering on her with affection. "Once you internalize that, navigating becomes second nature." "Indro," Tasha began, her brow furrowed in contemplation, "I understand the concept of fixed cardinal points, but without a compass, how can I determine which way is north while we're walking through the city?"

Indro smiled, appreciating her curiosity. "There are several methods to find north without a compass, even in an urban environment. One practical technique involves using an analog watch and the position of the sun."

"An analog watch?" Tasha echoed, glancing at her wrist adorned with a classic timepiece.

"mmhm", "Here's how it works: Hold your watch horizontally and point the hour hand directly at the sun. Look at the angle formed between the hour hand and the 12 o'clock mark on your watch. The line that bisects this angle indicates the north-south line. In the Northern Hemisphere, such as here in Mumbai, the sun is due south at noon. Therefore, the bisecting line's direction closer to the sun points south, and the opposite direction points north."

Tasha's eyes lit up with understanding. "So, by using my watch and the sun's position, I can establish the north-south line without a compass."

"Exactly," Indro replied, pleased with his explanation of the concept. "But Indro, how can I accurately point the hour hand at the sun without staring directly at it? Isn't that harmful?"

Indro nodded, acknowledging her concern. "You're right; looking directly at the sun can damage your eyes. Instead, use the shadow method: place a stick or any straight object upright on the ground. The shadow it casts will point directly away from the sun. Align your watch's hour hand with the shadow's direction, and then proceed to bisect the angle between the hour hand and the 12 o'clock mark to find the north-south line."

Tasha glanced at her watch, then at the ground, mentally practicing the method. "Thanks, Indro. With this, I feel more confident navigating without a compass."

"Anytime," Indro replied warmly. "It's always good to have a few tricks up your sleeve."

Their path led them past a familiar landmark—a puncture repair stall that had long been a fixture of the neighborhood. Or rather, what remained of it. The makeshift shack had been all but washed away by the rains, leaving behind a solitary yellow tire hanging from a tree branch, swaying gently in the breeze.

Tasha paused, her gaze fixed on the forlorn tire. "It's heartbreaking, isn't it? Your garden is flooded, but for someone like Raju, this is his entire livelihood gone."

Indro nodded solemnly. "The monsoon doesn't discriminate, but its impact is felt differently across the spectrum."

Tasha sighed, her thoughts drifting to the countless street vendors whose lives were upended by the seasonal deluge. "I read somewhere that during heavy rains, people remove manhole covers to divert excess water, but it often leads to accidents. Indro raised an eyebrow. "Yes, and sometimes thieves steal the manhole covers and sell them off in scrap markets. The BMC is trying to tackle the problem of stolen manhole covers."

Tasha shook her head, a mixture of frustration and empathy in her eyes. "It's a vicious cycle. The very measures people take to cope with the monsoon end up creating new hazards."

Indro glanced at the yellow tire, a symbol of resilience amidst adversity. "And yet, every year, the city bounces back. Streets are repaired, businesses reopen, and life goes on."

Tasha smiled softly. "Mumbai's indomitable spirit. It's what makes this city so unique."

As they continued their walk, a comfortable silence enveloped them. She marveled at his vast reservoir of knowledge, finding his explanations both enlightening and endearing. He, in turn, admired her ability to find beauty and meaning in the simplest of things—a quality he often felt eluded him. Each harbored a quiet wish to embody a bit more of the other's perspective: she yearned for his analytical clarity, while he longed for her unbridled joie de vivre. And so, with unspoken mutual respect, they walked on, their footsteps harmonizing with the gentle rhythm of the post-monsoon world around them.

As they turned a corner, a small, scruffy cat appeared, its fur matted from the recent downpour. It trotted up to them with a tentative flick of its tail, as if seeking companionship. She knelt down, extending a hand, and the cat nuzzled it affectionately. He watched with a smile as she scratched the cat's ears, her face lighting up with delight.

"Looks like we've made a new friend," she said, glancing up at him.

"Indeed," he replied. "I suppose you'll be calling him Nugget?"

She grinned. "You know me too well."

And so, with Nugget trotting happily beside them, they continued their journey, the trio embodying a harmonious blend of curiosity, wonder, and newfound friendship.

As they sloshed through a particularly puddle-ridden stretch of Juhu, Indro shifted the borrowed pump uncomfortably between his hands. His satchel, perpetually overstuffed, swung precariously from one shoulder. Amidst the rhythm of their steps, a familiar sound interrupted Tasha's monsoon musings.

"Is that...?" she began, turning toward the unmistakable shhk-shhk of Indro unscrewing his protein shaker.

"It's a long walk," he said defensively, tipping the shaker back for a sip. "And hydration is key."

Tasha raised an eyebrow. "Hydration, sure. But chocolate protein in the middle of a flood? That's a bold choice."

"You wouldn't understand," Indro replied with the smugness of someone entirely confident in their life choices. "This is what separates the disciplined from the—"

At that moment, his foot landed on what seemed like solid ground but was, in fact, an ancient, waterlogged manhole cover. It wobbled under his weight, and before he could react, the laws of physics took over. The pump tipped one way, Indro another, and the protein shaker—bless its sturdy design—shot its contents upward like a chocolate geyser.

The liquid arced gracefully through the air before landing with precision: a generous dollop on Indro's rain-drenched kurta, a mist of cocoa splatter on Tasha's cheek, and the remainder pooling mournfully in a nearby puddle.

For a moment, there was silence, save for the patter of rain and the gentle ripple of the chocolate puddle.

"Well," Tasha said finally, wiping a streak of protein from her face with exaggerated care. "I suppose we're calling that the Juhu Shake Disaster of 2024?"

Indro glared at the now-empty shaker as though it had betrayed him. "I don't know what's worse—the wasted protein or the ruined kurta."

"The kurta," Tasha said, smirking. "The protein was a lost cause the moment you decided to drink it mid-monsoon. Have you learned nothing from the Colaba Incident?"

Indro groaned, futilely dabbing at his shirt. "Why do these things always happen to me?"

"Because," Tasha replied, adopting her best sage-like tone, "Mumbai demands humility. And nothing humbles you faster than spilled protein."

Incredibly, a curious stall emerged from the misty drizzle. Perched precariously on stacked milk crates and secured with bungee cords to a lamppost, it looked more like an art experiment than a legitimate business. Above it, a sign made from pool floaties spelled out, "Paresh Puddle Wala's Waterproof Wonders," with a jaunty tilt that suggested either creativity or desperation.

Paresh himself, a bulging man with a raincoat patched in places that shouldn't have been patched, greeted them with an open smile. He waved enthusiastically, his hair plastered to his forehead. "Looking for something to keep the monsoon at bay? I've got the best of the worst, all right here!"

"What exactly is all this?" Indro asked, eyeing the chaotic assortment of wares—a tangle of snorkels, ponchos, and what appeared to be flip-flops fitted with ping-pong balls.

Paresh leaned forward conspiratorially, his grin widening. "Monsoon essentials, my friend. Anti-Pothole Floaters, Flood-Ready Slippers, and—my personal favourite—Puddle-Proof Cat Carriers." He pointed proudly to a box with a clear plastic dome attached, which looked like something a hamster might travel in.

At this, Nugget, tucked comfortably in Tasha's arms, flicked his tail with studied disdain, as if to say, how very plebeian.

"And the sign?" Tasha asked, smirking. "It looks like something from a carnival."

"Ah, yes," Paresh said, adjusting the floaties proudly. "Got the idea from an art exhibition at the Bandra gallery last month. All about upcycling, using trash to make a point about pollution. Thought I'd try my hand at it—gave it a bit of a monsoon twist, of course."

"Upcycling pool floaties into... advertising," Tasha mused. "Bold."

"Bold is the only way to survive the rain," Paresh replied. "You think I can compete with the big shops? Nah, I go for the laugh first. If people laugh, they stay, and if they stay, they buy." He tapped his forehead with a soggy finger. "Strategy, you see."

Nugget reached out a cautious paw toward a pair of fluorescent flip-flops dangling from the counter, setting them swinging. Indro chuckled. "Looks like you've got an endorsement."

"A cat with taste!" Paresh exclaimed. "You know, they always say dogs are loyal, but cats—they don't waste time. If they like you, you've earned it."

As the three prepared to leave, Indro glanced back. "Ever thought of turning this into a proper installation?"

Paresh grinned. "Every monsoon is an installation in this city, bhai. You've just got to learn to float through it."

Laughing, they moved on, Nugget now perched regally on Tasha's shoulder, casting a superior glance back at the stall. Paresh's ramshackle enterprise stayed with them, a testament to the city's ingenuity, humor, and refusal to sink under the weight of its own chaos.

As Indro and Tasha sloshed through the flooded lane, Nugget perched on Tasha's shoulder, ears flicking as though unimpressed with the weather, they spotted a woman wrestling with her bicycle under a dripping gulmohar tree. She was furiously trying to free the hem of her rain jacket, which had tangled with her chain. The entire scene had the air of someone trying to win an arm-wrestling match with a particularly stubborn octopus.

"Need a hand?" Indro called out, stepping carefully to avoid an unseen pothole.

She looked up, rainwater dripping from the edge of her helmet. "Do I look like I've got this under control?"

Tasha stifled a laugh as Indro reached into his pocket, producing a handkerchief. "This might help."

The woman took it, giving him a grateful smile. "You're a lifesaver. I'm Feroza, by the way—cyclist, monsoon survivor, and apparently, amateur mechanic."

"Indro. This is Tasha, and that's Nugget," he said, nodding at the cat, who stared at Feroza with the cool disdain only a stray cat-turned-royalty could muster.

Feroza cocked an eyebrow. "A cat? During the monsoon? And on foot?"

"Nugget adopted us," Tasha explained, adjusting the cat's position on her shoulder. "We didn't have much say in the matter. He follows me everywhere. Frankly, I think he likes the chaos."

Feroza chuckled, now kneeling to fix her chain. "A creature after my own heart. So, what's brought you two out into this aquatic wonderland?"

Indro sighed dramatically. "We're on a noble quest. My uncle's garden is currently auditioning to be Mumbai's newest lake. We're off to rent a pump."

"Ah, the joys of suburban flooding," Feroza said, standing as she wiped her hands on the handkerchief. She grimaced as she noticed a dark smear. "Sorry about this. I think your handkerchief just got promoted to 'rag.'"

"Keep it," Indro said generously. "It's now seen more action than I ever intended."

They began walking together, their feet sloshing in unison. Nugget flicked his tail as Feroza pushed her bike beside them, her rain jacket swishing like a reluctant sail.

"You know," she said, glancing at the water pooling in the cracks of the road, "I once hit a pothole on this very lane. I went flying—like Bollywood, slow-motion, DDLJ climax flying—straight into someone's vegetable cart."

Tasha burst out laughing. "What happened?"

"Oh, the cart survived. My dignity didn't. I smelled like coriander for a week," Feroza said, grinning. "The problem is, there's no map for these things. Every monsoon, the roads reinvent themselves. Potholes come and go like seasonal trends."

"And traffic?" Indro asked.

"Don't get me started," Feroza said. "Last week, I saw a rickshaw take what I can only describe as a leap of faith into a flooded street. The driver had no idea how deep it was. Turned out to be a pothole big enough to host a family of turtles."

"Cyclists must have it rough," Tasha said.

Feroza nodded fervently. "Oh, it's a game of survival. Motorists think cycle lanes are decorative. And pedestrians? They're too busy dodging the open drains. Once, a biker swerved so close I could feel the breeze. When I yelled, he actually shouted back, 'Aunty, this is Mumbai. Adjust!'"

Indro nearly choked on laughter. "Classic."

Feroza sighed, though she was still smiling. "Cycling here is like being in a live-action video game. You dodge potholes, weave through auto-rickshaws, and pray the monsoon doesn't throw in a bonus challenge like a landslide."

They approached a chai stall, where the chaiwallah gestured toward his steaming kettle. "Chai?" he offered.

"Never say no to chai," Feroza said, parking her bike.

As they sipped their tea, the chaiwallah casually tossed a bucket of soapy water into the nearby drain, causing it to bubble ominously. The murky liquid spilled back onto the road, mixing with the floodwater. "Civic efficiency at its finest," Feroza said, waving at the bubbling drain like it was an old friend. "Our sewage system's motto must be: 'Why fix it when you can just hope for the best?'"

Indro laughed. "You really stay cheerful through all this."

Feroza shrugged. "What choice do we have? The rains will flood, the roads will crumble, and cyclists like me will keep pedalling. It's Mumbai's way of reminding you to have a sense of humour—or else drown in your own misery."

As they finished their tea and prepared to part ways, Feroza waved a mock salute. "Good luck with the pump and tell Nugget I expect him to write a travelogue about his adventures."

"He'll dictate," Tasha quipped, patting the cat. "I'll type."

And with that, they splashed off in opposite directions, Feroza pedalling into the rain with the same tenacity she brought to everything, leaving Indro and Tasha with lighter hearts—and wet socks.

As Indro and Tasha trudged onward, Nugget balanced precariously on Tasha's shoulder, they rounded a corner onto a narrow lane, only to stop in their tracks. In the middle of the flooded road, a group of laborers was knee-deep in foul water, their hands busy with long bamboo poles as they struggled to unclog a drain.

The water shimmered with an oily sheen, and despite the relentless rain, the labourers were soaked in sweat from their exertions. A bystander, arms crossed, offered his unsolicited wisdom: "Use a longer stick! You have to scare the blockage into moving!"

"Clearly, a philosopher," Indro muttered, eliciting a snort from Tasha.

The laborers were working with grim determination, their footwear either nonexistent or makeshift—plastic bags tied around their ankles with twine. There wasn't a shred of protective gear in sight. One of them, a wiry man with a sun-darkened face, heaved his bamboo pole with a strength that belied his frame.

"Is this really the best way to clear it?" Tasha asked him as they passed.

He glanced up briefly. "Madam, you have better ideas?" he asked with a wry grin. "If someone lent us a proper pump or gloves, maybe. But this is what we have."

Nearby, a teenager holding a tiffin box for one of the workers chimed in. "My dad's been doing this for 15 years. He says if you hesitate, the water wins."

"And how often does it get this bad?" Tasha asked, her voice soft.

The teenager shrugged. "Every monsoon, same story. Water comes, drains choke, people call us. Sometimes, we get tea. Mostly, we don't."

As they moved further, Indro shook his head. "Makes you wonder if the city itself forgets the rains are annual."

"Forget the city," Tasha replied. "If half the people who threw garbage into drains offered these workers gloves, or even help directing traffic, it would make a difference."

They hadn't gone far when Tasha's phone buzzed. She pulled it out, wiping away raindrops, and scrolled through the news. "Well, the plot thickens," she said, showing Indro a photo of Andheri's infamous subway, now completely submerged.

A stranded commuter stood atop his stationary scooter, yelling at no one in particular, while a delivery man stood in waist-deep water, balancing a parcel on his head. According to the report, the delivery guy had flagged down an auto driver and handed him the parcel. The auto driver, undeterred by the flood, had made the delivery while the app still showed the order as "in transit."

"Creative problem-solving," Indro remarked. "Though I bet the delivery guy didn't explain why he was stuck."

"Can you blame him?" Tasha said. "He'd probably get a bad review if the samosas were soggy."

They continued walking, soon finding themselves in another jam—this one literal. A cluster of stalled vehicles clogged the road, drivers leaning out of windows to shout conflicting advice.

"Turn left!"

"There is no left!"

"Then go back, yaar!"

A young couple, stranded in a hatchback, used the downtime to take selfies against the backdrop of floating debris. Not far from them, an elderly man waved his umbrella like a general commanding troops, directing a bus driver to reverse into slightly shallower water. Miraculously, it worked.

"You know," Indro observed, "if everyone worked together like that, this city might actually survive monsoon season unscathed."

"Dream on," Tasha replied. "The guy in the Audi over there just revved his engine and splashed an entire family on the footpath."

"Fine," Indro conceded. "Two steps forward, one giant splash back."

As they pressed on, dodging puddles and errant vehicles, Tasha glanced back at the laborers. "Makes you think, doesn't it? About all the invisible people who keep this city going."

"And all the visible ones who make it harder," Indro added. Nugget, perched on Tasha's shoulder, flicked his tail like a metronome of disapproval, his fur fluffed into what could only be described as a monsoon scowl.

"Do you think Nugget will sue us for emotional distress after this?" Indro asked, glancing at the cat.

Tasha grinned. "Only if he learns to use Google Forms."

They turned onto a street that seemed to be auditioning for a National Geographic feature on urban flooding. The water rippled ominously, and just as Tasha opened her mouth to comment, Nugget leapt off her shoulder and landed deftly on a dry-ish patch of pavement, staring at the ground with laser-like focus.

"What's he—" Indro began but stopped when the water in front of them gave a sinister gurgle. Nugget hissed and bolted back to Tasha just as the surface gave way, revealing a pothole large enough to house a small scooter—and possibly its rider.

Tasha peered into the abyss. "That's not a pothole. That's a real estate opportunity."

Indro laughed, shaking his head. "Can you imagine if they started charging rent for potholes? Prime locations on Linking Road would go for a fortune."

"You could even Airbnb it," Tasha added, her voice mock-serious. "'Charming water feature, comes with built-in mosquito farm.'"

They gingerly navigated around the pothole and pressed on. Indro pulled out his phone to check the weather. "Look at this," he said, holding the screen up to Tasha. "No rain predicted for the next six hours. The sun is supposed to make a heroic return."

At that precise moment, as if summoned by some celestial sense of irony, the sky opened up with a roar and unleashed a torrent of rain so intense it felt personal. Indro stared at his phone in disbelief. "I think the weather app just gaslit me."

Tasha, who had stopped to shield Nugget under her jacket, shook her head. "What's the point of all this technology if it can't predict the one thing this city is famous for? They might as well replace these apps with a disclaimer: 'Rain is always a possibility. Good luck.'

As the rain intensified, they stumbled upon a gated compound where the security guard was lounging under a dry overhang, sipping tea. Nugget wriggled out of Tasha's hold and darted under the shelter, meowing as though filing a formal complaint about their parenting skills.

"Can you keep him here for a bit?" Tasha asked the guard, motioning to the cat. "Just until the rain stops?"

The guard looked down at Nugget, who was now sitting primly as if auditioning for the role of "Most Regal Street Cat in Mumbai." He chuckled. "Of course, madam. I'll give him some biscuits too."

Tasha turned to Nugget. "Stay here, okay? Be good. Don't unionize with the other strays."

Nugget blinked slowly, the universal feline signal for I acknowledge you but remain sovereign.

With one last look at their now-sheltered companion, Tasha and Indro stepped back into the downpour, leaving Nugget behind to charm his new caretaker and enjoy the luxury of being dry for the first time that day.

The rain fell with an unrelenting fury, drenching Indro and Tasha as they carefully navigated what could only be described as a watery obstacle course. The street ahead shimmered like a deceptively calm lake, interrupted by ripples every time a hapless pedestrian ventured too far into the depths.

"Behold," Indro declared, gesturing grandly to the scene ahead. "Mumbai's newest tourist attraction: The Great Urban Lagoon. Watch your step—it comes with complimentary surprises."

The surprises, of course, were the potholes. Each one lurked beneath the water like a mischievous creature waiting to pounce. As Tasha stepped forward, Nugget, now temporarily safe with a security guard, was no longer around to warn her. Her foot sank abruptly into what she assumed was solid ground.

"Whoa!" she yelped, flailing for balance as Indro grabbed her arm just in time to save her from a full-body baptism. "What was that? A sinkhole?"

"No," Indro said gravely, peering into the abyss. "That's a pothole. Or, as we like to call them, Mumbai's surprise party for pedestrians."

Nearby, a cyclist wobbled precariously before his front wheel disappeared into a hidden pothole. He flipped forward in a slow-motion somersault, landing on his feet like an unplanned circus act. The small crowd watching burst into applause as if this were an intentional performance.

"Ten points for grace!" someone shouted.

The cyclist, dripping but dignified, gave a mock bow before retrieving his bike and muttering about "revenge on the municipality."

As Indro and Tasha moved on, a rickshaw splashed by, its front wheel catching in another pothole. The driver leaned out, yelling, "Arey, who put this manhole here?" to no one in particular, as though expecting a personal apology from the rain gods.

"Imagine trying to explain this to a tourist," Tasha said, shaking her head. "'It's not a defect; it's a feature. Builds character!'"

"Or fitness," Indro added, watching a man leap nimbly from one dry spot to another, his movements a perfect imitation of an Olympic long-jumper.

A few streets later, they encountered what looked like the aftermath of a shipwreck. Cars were stalled in every direction, their drivers stranded atop roofs and hoods like castaways. A bus sat at a precarious tilt, its back half submerged, while passengers pressed against the windows, debating whether escape was worth the swim.

But amidst the chaos, something remarkable was unfolding. A group of strangers had linked hands, forming a human chain to guide an elderly couple across the flooded street. The current threatened to sweep them off their feet, but the chain held firm, each person bracing against the force for the one beside them.

"Look at that," Tasha said, her voice tinged with admiration. "Mumbai's finest at work."

The human chain extended to help a delivery boy carrying a tower of tiffin boxes on his head. As he crossed, balancing like a tightrope walker, someone in the chain shouted, "Careful, yaar! Those are my wife's rotis—don't let them get wet!"

Laughter rippled through the group, the moment of levity somehow making their effort even stronger.

On the far side of the chain, a woman in a saree had taken charge, barking orders like a general. "Hold on tightly! You there, stop giggling—this is serious work!" She tugged the arm of a teenager who was clearly enjoying the adventure a little too much. "And you—stop taking selfies!"

Indro leaned toward Tasha. "Do you think they'll take her for mayor after this?"

"Only if she promises to build bridges," Tasha replied, laughing.

As they stood watching, a man in a business suit stumbled out of the water, his tie plastered to his chest. He paused to join the chain, his polished shoes completely ruined but his spirit evidently intact.

"You have to admire this," Tasha said. "In any other city, people would stand around filming this on their phones. Here, they just jump in."

"Mostly," Indro replied. "Don't forget Mr. Selfie over there."

Together, they helped a mother with two toddlers join the human chain, the children giggling as though this were the greatest game they'd ever played. The chain grew longer, stronger, and by the time the worst of the water was crossed, it seemed like everyone involved was a little lighter for the experience.

"Maybe this city's chaos is its charm," Tasha mused as they walked on.

"Charm is one word for it," Indro said. "But I think it's just stubbornness. Mumbai doesn't break—it improvises."

And as they trudged forward, soaking wet but smiling, they couldn't help but feel that somehow, against all odds, the city always found a way to stay afloat.

Indro and Tasha waded through the flooded streets of Juhu, and their phones buzzed simultaneously. The previously unresponsive pump rental service had finally sent a message, complete with a live location pin.

"Look at that," Indro remarked, showing his screen to Tasha. "Our elusive pump has decided to make an appearance."

Tasha squinted at the map. "It's at the community center on Gulmohar Road. That's not too far."

They adjusted their course, navigating through the watery maze. The rain had transformed familiar streets into unpredictable channels, with submerged potholes lying in wait like urban traps. Each step was a cautious gamble, the murky water concealing potential hazards.

As they approached Gulmohar Road, the scene shifted. The community center stood as a beacon of organized chaos. Residents bustled about, coordinating efforts to combat the encroaching water. Buckets were passed in assembly lines, and makeshift barriers were erected to divert the flow.

"Impressive," Tasha observed. "Looks like the neighborhood took matters into their own hands."

Indro nodded. "When official channels fail, grassroots ingenuity steps up."

They made their way to the main hall, where a group of volunteers was gathered around a dewatering pump. The machine hummed steadily, siphoning water with determined efficiency.

A middle-aged woman with a clipboard approached them. "You must be here for the pump," she said, her tone brisk but friendly.

"Yes," Indro replied. "We called earlier but couldn't get through."

The woman sighed. "Apologies for that. Our lines have been overwhelmed. We decided to pool our resources and rent this pump collectively. It's been a lifeline for the neighborhood."

Tasha glanced around at the coordinated effort. "It's heartening to see such community spirit."

The woman smiled. "In times like these, we can't wait for help to arrive. We have to be the help."

After coordinating with the volunteers, Indro and Tasha arranged to borrow the pump for Sundar Niket. With the machine secured, they began their journey back, the weight of the equipment balanced between them.

As they retraced their steps, the city's resilience was on full display. Neighbors shared umbrellas, strangers offered helping hands, and makeshift signs warned of hidden dangers beneath the water's surface.

"Despite all the challenges," Tasha mused, "there's an undeniable strength in this city's people."

Indro nodded. "It's a place where adversity brings out the best in everyone."

Back at Sundar Niket, they set up the pump, and soon, the garden began to drain. As the water receded, so did the tension that had gripped them.

"Today was quite the adventure," Tasha remarked, wiping her brow.

Indro chuckled. "Just another day in Mumbai during the monsoon."

They stood together, watching as the last of the floodwater was expelled, a sense of accomplishment settling over them. In the face of nature's fury and infrastructural shortcomings, the spirit of community had prevailed, turning a daunting ordeal into a testament to human resilience.

Chapter 9

Mastery of Meaning

The SUV sat like a battle-ready beast on the cobblestones of Horniman Circle, its glossy black surface reflecting the dappled morning light filtering through the leafy trees. Tasha adjusted her sunglasses—a flamboyant cat-eye pair that seemed to scream, "I mean business"—and tapped her fingers impatiently on the steering wheel. The air inside the car was a crisp mix of coffee aroma from the travel mugs and faint anticipation for the adventure ahead.

"You do realize," Indro began, lounging in the passenger seat with the practiced air of someone about to deliver a lecture, "that this is the calmest moment we're going to have all day?"

"Which is why I'm savouring it," Tasha replied, stretching her neck theatrically like a boxer before a match. "Mumbai traffic has nothing on me. I'm the queen of manoeuvring. A maestro of lane-switching."

Indro raised an eyebrow and looked pointedly at the rearview mirror. "Yes, the last time you said that, you mistook a no-entry for a shortcut. How'd that work out?"

Tasha waved him off. "Details, details. Besides, that was a strategic miscalculation. We arrived five minutes earlier, didn't we?"

"And nearly ran over a pani puri vendor in the process," Indro muttered under his breath.

The SUV purred to life, its engine growling softly as Tasha eased it forward, commanding immediate respect from the pedestrians and errant cyclists. She tilted her head toward the majestic Asiatic Society Library, its pristine white columns glowing in the morning sun.

"Look at that," Indro said, gesturing with his travel mug. "Built in 1804. It's older than the first train in this city. Those columns have seen revolutions, riots, and the rise of Instagram."

Tasha gave it a quick glance as she turned the wheel with deliberate grace. "I'll admit it's impressive. But you know what would be even more impressive? Parking. You can preserve a building but can't spare a square foot for my SUV."

"Parking," Indro repeated, taking a long sip of his coffee, "isn't a problem. It's an art form. A survival skill. A metaphor for life in Mumbai."

"Spoken like a man who's never parallel-parked a tank," Tasha retorted, referring to her SUV. She adjusted the AC, the cool air brushing away the faint humidity that had started to creep in.

As the car rolled past the library, a stray dog ambled lazily across the cobblestones, pausing to sniff a discarded samosa wrapper. Tasha hit the brakes gently, her reflexes sharp.

"See? Queen of navigating," she said with a smirk. "Flawless. Elegant."

Indro shook his head. "Give it time. We haven't even hit the real chaos yet."

"Chaos," Tasha replied, accelerating smoothly, "is where I thrive. This city and I have an understanding. It throws me roadblocks; I throw it back sass."

They turned onto the main road, the SUV's elevated seating giving them a clear view of the bustle ahead. Street vendors were setting up stalls, their brightly colored umbrellas dotting the sidewalks like a mosaic. A cluster of office workers jostled near a bus stop, their chatter blending into the city's symphony of honks and whistles.

"So, enlighten me," Tasha said, glancing sideways at Indro. "What's the deal with this library? What makes it so special?"

Indro leaned back, adopting the tone of a university lecturer. "The Asiatic Society houses over a hundred thousand books, including some of the rarest manuscripts. Imagine holding a piece of history in your hands—a document written centuries ago, surviving wars, plagues, and bad governance."

Tasha raised an eyebrow. "And imagine trying to find parking while you hold this piece of history."

He ignored her. "Do you know they have original copies of Dante's Divine Comedy? And the original manuscript of Shah Jahan's Chronicles?"

"That's nice," Tasha said dryly. "Does it include tips on where to park your SUV without getting towed?"

Indro sighed dramatically. "This is why I can't discuss literature with you. No appreciation for the finer things."

"No," Tasha corrected, weaving expertly around a cyclist who had suddenly decided to occupy the middle of the lane, "I have appreciation. I just prefer my finer things to come with valet service."

The SUV picked up speed, leaving the quiet dignity of Horniman Circle behind. The city stretched out ahead, a cacophony of sounds, colours, and unpredictable movements. Tasha adjusted her grip on the wheel, her eyes scanning the road like a hawk surveying its territory.

"You know," she said after a pause, "I think libraries could learn a thing or two from coffee shops."

Indro gave her a puzzled look. "Coffee shops?"

"Yeah," she said, grinning. "Make them cozy. Add couches. Offer good chai and Wi-Fi. Suddenly, you'd have millennials lined up outside, fighting over books instead of TikTok trends."

Indro considered this. "It's an intriguing idea. But I think you underestimate the allure of dust-covered classics and bad lighting. It's part of the charm."

"Charm," Tasha repeated, snorting. "That's just code for, 'We don't have a budget.'"

The SUV cruised out of Horniman Circle, its elevated stance giving Tasha a sense of command over the morning bustle. They were headed toward Marine Drive, the city's iconic promenade, but the journey, as always, was bound to be riddled with its own set of Mumbai-specific absurdities.

As they approached the turn for Princess Street Flyover, Tasha slowed down, scanning the road signs with a scrutinizing glare.

"Marine Drive ⊠ | Chowpatty ⊠"

She raised an eyebrow and muttered, "So, do we go straight or take the flyover to nowhere?"

Indro adjusted his seatbelt, sipping his coffee with maddening calmness. "Mumbai signage doesn't give answers. It asks questions. Existential ones."

"Like whether I'll live to see my destination?" Tasha quipped, gripping the steering wheel tighter.

"Precisely," Indro said. "Or whether the destination even exists. Maybe Marine Drive is just a state of mind."

Tasha rolled her eyes and chose the most promising lane. Her SUV made a smooth but assertive turn onto Marine Drive, only narrowly avoiding a rickshaw with a penchant for last-second lane changes.

"You see that?" Tasha said, gesturing toward the rickshaw. "That man's entire life flashed before his eyes, and he still didn't use his indicator."

"Indicators are for the weak," Indro replied. "True Mumbai drivers navigate by intuition, muscle memory, and sheer audacity."

The sea came into view as they hit the stretch of Marine Drive, a sweeping curve that hugged the Arabian coastline. Palm trees lined the promenade, and the waves sparkled under the late morning sun, offering a serene contrast to the chaos of the traffic.

"Ah," Indro said, leaning back. "The Queen's Necklace. Glittering proof that Mumbai occasionally remembers how to dazzle."

"It's pretty," Tasha admitted, her tone softening for a moment. "But do you know what it's missing?"

"More signs pointing to nowhere?" Indro offered.

"No," Tasha said, a grin forming on her face. "Fewer people blasting Punjabi remixes out of their hatchbacks."

As if on cue, a car pulled up next to them at a red light, windows down and speakers blaring. The bass reverberated through the SUV's interior, shaking their coffee mugs. Tasha winced, rolling up her windows in defeat.

"This city," she said, "has no respect for personal space. Even sound waves don't respect boundaries."

Indro shrugged. "Maybe they're just spreading joy. Or trying to make sure we all know the lyrics to Brown Munde."

The light turned green, and Tasha accelerated, leaving the music far behind. She stole a glance at the promenade, where joggers weaved between families taking leisurely strolls. Vendors were setting up stalls selling roasted peanuts, their carts painted in cheerful hues of yellow and red.

"It's funny," Tasha said, her tone turning reflective. "This place is so chaotic, but when you look at the sea, it all feels… manageable. Like the waves are whispering, 'Don't worry, I've seen worse.'"

"That's deep," Indro said, looking genuinely impressed. "The waves as Mumbai's silent therapists. You could write poetry."

"I could also write a manual on how to survive Mumbai's roads," she shot back. "Chapter One: Honk First, Think Later."

They both laughed, but the conversation took a turn toward introspection as Indro gazed at the sea. "Do you think the city is kind to anyone?" he asked suddenly.

Tasha considered this. "Kind? No. Fair? Absolutely not. But it's generous in weird ways. It teaches you patience. Resilience. And how to dodge potholes like a pro."

"That's oddly optimistic," Indro said, surprised.

"It's not optimism," Tasha corrected. "It's survival. And a little bit of Stockholm syndrome."

They drove in silence for a moment, the hum of the SUV's engine blending with the faint murmur of waves. Then, as they passed another road sign that appeared to offer two contradictory directions, Indro spoke again.

"You know, this reminds me of a story," he began, his tone shifting to that of a raconteur.

"Of course it does," Tasha said, rolling her eyes. "You're incapable of seeing a road sign without turning it into an anecdote."

"This one's worth it," Indro promised. "There was this friend of mine—Rohan. Got a fancy new job and decided to take his dad for a drive to celebrate. They wanted to go to Chowpatty, so naturally, they followed the signs."

"And?" Tasha asked, already sensing the punchline.

"And they ended up at the airport. Apparently, he missed the tiny sign that said, 'Keep Right.' His dad didn't speak to him for a week."

Tasha burst out laughing. "Classic. That's so… Mumbai. A city that promises you the beach and delivers you to Departures."

"Exactly," Indro said, grinning. "It's a metaphor for life here. You think you're heading somewhere peaceful, but you always end up in chaos."

As they approached Chowpatty, the aroma of street food wafted into the SUV despite the closed windows. The sight of bhel puri vendors setting up their carts made Tasha's stomach growl.

"Feel like stopping for a snack?" she asked.

"Not unless you want to risk losing the parking spot of a lifetime," Indro replied. "This is Mumbai. You park, you pay."

"Pay with your soul," Tasha agreed, accelerating smoothly past the tempting stalls. Indro leaned back, cradling his protein shaker like a prized artifact. The traffic ahead crawled to a stop, and he seized the moment to unscrew the lid with a flourish.

Tasha gave him a side-eye glance. "You do realize we're in a moving vehicle surrounded by potholes the size of small lakes?"

"Correction," Indro said smugly, taking a sip. "We're in your expertly driven vehicle. I trust you implicitly."

"That," Tasha replied, flicking on the indicator, "is your first mistake."

Before Indro could formulate a comeback, Tasha swerved to avoid a scooter that had materialized out of nowhere, its rider inexplicably balancing a stack of empty gas cylinders. It was flawless—poetry in motion, some might say—but it sent the contents of Indro's shaker into a decidedly unpoetic trajectory.

A wave of chocolatey liquid arced through the air, landing with deadly precision on the dashboard, Tasha's sunglasses, and, most tragically, her pristine white scarf.

For a moment, there was silence, broken only by the rhythmic honking of a bus behind them.

"Indro," Tasha said, her voice dangerously calm. "Did you just baptize my car with protein shake?"

Indro blinked at her, still holding the shaker, now pathetically empty. "I… I think the lid was loose."

"The lid was loose," Tasha repeated, peeling the sticky scarf off her neck like a surgeon removing contaminated gloves. "And yet, you thought this was the time for a drink?"

"Well," Indro began, his tone sheepish, "hydration is—"

"Don't," Tasha interrupted, holding up a chocolate-smeared hand. "Do not say 'hydration is key.'"

Indro cleaned up the dashboard frantically. "Sorry, I admit it. I miscalculated. Can we move on?"

Tasha, now halfway through salvaging her scarf, glanced at him. "Oh, we'll move on. But you're buying me a new scarf."

The SUV continued its journey along Marine Drive, its occupants alternating between laughter, reflection, and the occasional muttered curse at an errant scooter. The sea watched silently, as if amused by their antics, a constant reminder that in this city of dreams, survival was its own kind of art.

The SUV merged onto the newly constructed Coastal Road, a gleaming stretch of concrete cutting across reclaimed land, bordered on one side by the Arabian Sea and on the other by the burgeoning skyline. The air of novelty hung thick, as if the road itself was unsure about its place in the chaos of Mumbai.

"This is it!" Tasha exclaimed, her hands gripping the wheel with theatrical excitement. "The future of Mumbai. Look at this beauty—smooth, wide, no potholes. I could cry."

"Hold those tears," Indro said, scrolling through his phone. "Let's see if we even survive this 'trial run.' It's technically not open yet. We might be trespassing."

Tasha shrugged. "A minor detail. Progress doesn't wait for permission."

Indro smirked. "Neither do Mumbai drivers, apparently. I'm sure we'll have company soon."

As they cruised along, the sea glistened in the late-morning sun, waves breaking gently against the barriers. The road was eerily quiet compared to the usual Mumbai din. Tasha couldn't resist pressing the accelerator a little harder, feeling the SUV glide effortlessly.

"This," she declared, "is what liberation feels like. No traffic, no honking, just me, my SUV, and the open road."

Indro leaned back, taking in the view. "You know, this stretch reminds me of the David Sassoon Library."

Tasha raised an eyebrow. "How does a brand-new expressway remind you of a 19th-century Gothic library?"

"Well," Indro began, his tone taking on the air of a storyteller, "the David Sassoon Library was completed in 1870, funded by one of Mumbai's most philanthropic families. It's a Grade I heritage structure, with those iconic pointed arches and stained glass. A true architectural marvel."

"Lovely," Tasha said, feigning interest. "But what's the connection?"

Indro gestured out the window. "Both are ambitious projects meant to elevate Mumbai. Both serve as symbols of progress, but both also face the same problem—maintenance. This road might look pristine today, but give it a monsoon or two, and we'll be back to dodging craters."

Tasha laughed. "True. It's like Mumbai is allergic to things staying intact. Even history."

"And that's the tragedy," Indro continued, his tone more reflective now. "These architectural gems, like the David Sassoon Library, survive centuries, but urban development threatens their very existence. It's ironic—progress consumes what it should preserve."

The SUV sped along a particularly picturesque stretch, where the sea appeared almost to touch the road. Tasha glanced sideways at Indro. "For someone who claims to love progress, you sound awfully nostalgic."

"I'm not against progress," Indro clarified. "I'm just against forgetting. Take the Mumbai Marathi Grantha Sangrahalaya, for instance. It's one of the oldest Marathi libraries in the city, but its membership has dropped from 11,000 to just 8,000 in the last decade."

"Why?" Tasha asked, genuinely curious.

"Lack of interest. Lack of funding. People don't see libraries as necessary anymore, not when you can Google everything or download e-books."

Tasha snorted. "Because nothing says intellectual like binge-watching conspiracy videos on YouTube."

"Exactly," Indro said, smirking. "And what's worse, the Sangrahalaya received just ₹34 lakh from the government last year—barely enough to keep the lights on, let alone modernize."

"That's depressing," Tasha said. "Libraries are supposed to be sanctuaries, not relics."

"Sanctuaries," Indro echoed. "That's a good word for it. But in Mumbai, they're becoming more like mausoleums. Places we visit to mourn what we've lost."

For a moment, the conversation lulled, replaced by the rhythmic hum of the SUV's tires against the smooth road. Then, as they approached an upcoming curve, they spotted a small sign that read:

"Caution: Unmarked Turns Ahead"

Tasha squinted. "Unmarked turns? That's not a warning; that's a philosophical dilemma."

"Welcome to Mumbai," Indro said dryly. "Where even the roads have trust issues."

She slowed down slightly, the SUV navigating the curve with ease. "You know," she said after a pause, "if libraries want to survive, they need to adapt. Make themselves irresistible. Like coffee shops."

Indro laughed. "So, you're saying libraries should serve overpriced lattes and have free Wi-Fi?"

"Exactly!" Tasha said. "Imagine it—curling up with a good book, a chai latte in hand, no one judging you for how long you stay. They could even let cats roam around for ambiance."

"Cats?" Indro asked, incredulous.

"Yeah," Tasha said, grinning. "Like Nugget. He'd make an excellent librarian—judgmental, aloof, but secretly helpful."

Indro shook his head, but he was smiling. "That might work. Though I don't think Nugget would tolerate late fees."

The SUV sped up again as they cleared the curve, the sea once more coming into full view. Despite the humour, both felt the weight of their discussion lingering in the air. Mumbai's libraries, like its roads, needed more than just plans and structures—they needed love, attention, and, perhaps, a little reinvention.

As Tasha maneuvered the SUV past the next signpost—"Haji Ali Dargah ← | Worli Sea Face →"—she braked slightly to assess the situation. A scooter zipped past her, narrowly missing the bumper.

"Ah, Mumbai drivers," she muttered, "taking Darwinism to a whole new level."

Indro glanced at the chaos unfolding outside. "Natural selection, but make it traffic."

Tasha rolled her eyes. "You know what's worse than Mumbai drivers?"

"What?"

"Signals. It's like a talent show for bad behaviour."

As if on cue, they hit a red light near Haji Ali Junction. Tasha brought the SUV to a smooth stop, but her peripheral vision caught something she wished she hadn't.

The man in the car beside them, seated in a gleaming white luxury sedan, had one finger buried unceremoniously up his nostril, his other hand casually draped over the steering wheel. His expression was one of deep concentration, as though the fate of humanity depended on his excavations.

Tasha slapped Indro's arm. "Look at that. A man with a million-dollar car and a zero-dollar sense of decorum."

Indro turned, grimaced, and then burst into laughter. "The digging! The precision! It's almost… artisanal."

"Do you think he's auditioning for a civic sense campaign?" Tasha deadpanned. "Because he's nailing the theme of irony."

Indro leaned closer to the window. "Or maybe it's a form of meditation. You know, find inner peace while mining for gold."

Tasha couldn't hold back her laughter. "Inner peace, sure. But what if he strikes oil?"

The light turned green, and the man sped off, leaving Tasha and Indro to ponder the spectacle.

As they continued toward Worli, Indro glanced out at the Haji Ali Dargah, its white marble structure shimmering against the backdrop of the sea.

"You know," he began, "this reminds me of something I saw at the Kala Ghoda Festival last year."

Tasha groaned. "Oh no. Here comes another one of your obscure connections."

"No, listen," Indro said, undeterred. "They had this art installation—a giant papier-mâché nose with little hands reaching out of it."

"What?" Tasha asked, incredulous.

"Swear to God," Indro replied, chuckling. "It was a commentary on public hygiene. Very avant-garde."

"Well, they should've invited our friend back there to be the muse," Tasha quipped, gesturing to where the luxury car had been.

The conversation shifted as they passed a banner advertising the Kala Ghoda Arts Festival. Brightly coloured illustrations of dancers, painters, and musicians adorned the signs.

"I love the festival," Tasha said. "It's chaotic, but in a good way. Unlike this traffic."

Indro nodded. "And the David Sassoon Library always looks like a star during the festival. Did you hear about the restoration?"

"I did," Tasha said. "Took over a year, but they've brought back all the intricate details—the arches, the stained glass, even the gargoyles."

"Speaking of restoration," Indro added, "I hope they restored the AC. The last time I visited, it felt like I was in a sauna with a thousand dusty books."

Tasha snorted. "They call it atmosphere. You call it poor ventilation."

Indro shrugged. "Details. But I will say, the Kala Ghoda Festival gives the whole area new life. It's like the city collectively remembers it has culture."

"And then promptly forgets it when the festival's over," Tasha retorted, honking lightly at a car that had decided to stop mid-road to buy a coconut.

As they approached another signal, Tasha sighed. "This city doesn't need more cars or more roads. It needs a crash course in civic sense."

Indro pointed to another vehicle where a man was leaning halfway out of his car window to spit. "Literally."

Tasha shook her head. "And we wonder why they call it Maximum City."

"Well," Indro said, smirking, "at least it's never boring."

The SUV rolled on, leaving behind the junction, but carrying the hilarity of Mumbai's uniquely unfiltered humanity with them.

The SUV hummed steadily as Tasha and Indro neared the Worli Sea Link, Mumbai's iconic bridge connecting two worlds—South Bombay's timeless chaos and the glimmering suburban sprawl of Bandra. The approach road was wide, clean, and shockingly devoid of potholes, which immediately made Tasha suspicious.

"I don't trust it," she muttered, gripping the wheel.

"Trust what?" Indro asked, lazily scrolling through his phone.

"This road. It's too smooth. Too perfect. It feels like a trap."

Indro laughed. "You've been in Mumbai too long. You can't accept something working properly without imagining doom."

She shot him a look but didn't argue. Her instincts as a Mumbaikar were rarely wrong. As they approached the signage for the Sea Link, she slowed the SUV, squinting at the green board overhead.

"BWSL Entry Ahead"

Tasha tapped the brakes. "That's it? That's all it says? No distance marker? No lane guidance? Just a vague promise of entry?"

Indro peered at the sign. "Minimalism. Mumbai's infrastructure is going through its Scandinavian design phase."

"Scandinavian? This is more like cryptic performance art," she shot back. "I half expect the next sign to just say, 'Good Luck.'"

She maneuvered the SUV carefully, her eyes darting between the merging lanes. Two cars ahead, a luxury sedan abruptly swerved left without signalling, narrowly missing a rickshaw that retaliated with a symphony of honks.

"Beautiful," Tasha muttered. "Look at that choreography. The Bolshoi Ballet wishes it had this kind of drama."

Indro was too busy watching the Sea Link rise in the distance, its elegant cables stretching into the sky. "You must admit, though, it's stunning. A literal bridge between chaos and calm."

"Don't romanticize it," Tasha said. "It's just a glorified shortcut for people who can afford the toll. You know what I think every time I see this thing?"

"What?"

"That they should've built a pedestrian lane. Imagine walking across this bridge. The sea breeze, the views, no honking—pure bliss."

"Until a cyclist decides to ride in the pedestrian lane," Indro countered. "And then it's back to chaos."

Tasha sighed. "Fine. I'll stick to my dream of a Mumbai where drivers use indicators."

They entered the Sea Link, the SUV's tires gliding over the pristine surface. The bridge arched gracefully over the Arabian Sea, offering a panoramic view of the city's skyline to their left and the endless expanse of water to their right. For a moment, even Tasha was quiet, her usual sharp wit giving way to quiet appreciation.

"Do you think," Indro began, breaking the silence, "if someone from 19th-century Mumbai saw this, they'd think we'd solved all our problems?"

Tasha considered it. "Probably. And then they'd take one look at the traffic under the bridge and think, 'Ah, never mind.'"

Indro chuckled, but his gaze lingered on the horizon. "It's funny, isn't it? How we build these marvels to rise above the mess, but the mess is still there, just out of sight."

"Very profound," Tasha said, glancing at him. "But I was promised no lofty metaphors today."

"Fine," he conceded, leaning back in his seat. "But let me say this: Mumbai is the only city where you can feel stuck and free at the same time."

She smirked. "Now that's a metaphor I'll allow."

As they neared the toll plaza, Tasha slowed down, her fingers drumming against the steering wheel. The Sea Link toll booths were an exercise in organized chaos. Each lane bore a sign: "FASTag Only," "Cash," "Mixed."

"Okay," she said, scanning the options. "Which one are we taking?"

"Depends," Indro replied. "Are we law-abiding citizens or opportunists?"

"Opportunists," Tasha decided, swerving into the 'Mixed' lane. A long queue stretched ahead, but she wasn't deterred.

The car in front of them—a sleek black sedan—refused to budge. The driver was apparently having a heated argument with the toll attendant.

"What's happening?" Indro asked, craning his neck.

Tasha leaned on the horn briefly. "Probably trying to pay with expired coupons or something equally idiotic."

Indro shook his head. "Do you think they argue this much in other cities?"

"No," she said. "In other cities, people have shame."

"Ah, but Mumbai," Indro said with mock reverence, "is a place where shame is considered a weakness. Here, the louder you argue, the more you win."

Eventually, the sedan moved, and Tasha paid the toll without incident. As they re-entered the bridge, she accelerated slightly, savouring the smoothness of the ride.

"You know," she said, "the Sea Link is like a good library."

"How so?" Indro asked.

"It's quiet, clean, and full of potential," she explained. "But not everyone can access it, and most people don't use it the way it's intended."

Indro laughed. "That's true. Though libraries don't charge you a toll for every visit."

"Maybe they should," Tasha said. "Use the money to fix their ACs."

Indro shook his head. "You'd turn libraries into private clubs."

"Why not?" she said, grinning. "At least it'd keep the riffraff out."

"And by riffraff, you mean people who can't afford your hypothetical toll?"

"Obviously," she said, laughing. "I'm a monster, not a socialist."

They continued over the Sea Link, the conversation flowing as easily as the road beneath them. The bridge stretched endlessly ahead, its cables glinting in the sun, and for a moment, it felt like the city's chaos was a world away.

The SUV approached the Sea Link toll plaza, where rows of booths and blinking lane markers promised some semblance of order—but not too much, lest anyone feel out of place. Tasha slowed down, her eyes narrowing as she scanned the options: "FASTag Only," "Cash," "Mixed."

"Why do they call it 'Mixed'?" she asked, drumming her fingers on the steering wheel. "It's not a cocktail bar."

"Mixed," Indro said, adjusting his seatbelt, "is where hopes and dreams go to die."

Tasha snorted, swerving confidently into the Mixed Lane. Ahead of them, a man in a beat-up hatchback seemed to be having a philosophical disagreement with the toll attendant. His arm flailed dramatically out of the window, clutching what looked like a faded receipt.

"What's the debate?" Indro asked, peering ahead.

"Probably trying to pay with Monopoly money," Tasha replied. "Or asking if the toll is included in his horoscope."

Indro grinned. "Or maybe he's arguing that his FASTag is fasting."

The hatchback finally moved, though not without a long, lingering honk of dissatisfaction. Tasha pulled up to the booth with the air of someone preparing for battle. She handed over the exact change and drove off before the attendant could utter a word.

"Efficiency," she said, nodding firmly. "That's how you handle a toll booth."

"Efficiency," Indro echoed, "or ruthlessness?"

"Both," she replied. "It's called multitasking."

Once back on the bridge, the Sea Link opened before them, and the SUV surged forward, its engine humming contentedly. Tasha's hands gripped the wheel with practiced confidence, her eyes scanning the road for any sudden surprises.

"You know," Indro said, breaking the silence, "this bridge kind of reminds me of a library."

Tasha raised an eyebrow. "The bridge reminds you of a library? Please explain, Socrates."

"Well," he said, leaning back in his seat, "it's quiet, structured, and full of potential. But only if you know how to use it."

Tasha smirked. "You're just making stuff up now."

"No, seriously," Indro insisted. "Take the People's Free Reading and Library. It's this unassuming little place, but it offers subsidized memberships and has entire sections dedicated to students."

"That's great," Tasha said, deftly switching lanes to overtake a truck. "Except most students these days are more likely to Google their homework than set foot in a library."

"True," Indro admitted. "But places like that still matter. They're like anchors—keeping communities grounded, even if people don't realize it."

"Anchors," Tasha repeated. "Nice metaphor. Maybe next you'll compare this bridge to a rare manuscript."

Indro grinned. "Funny you should mention that. The J. N. Petit Library has one of the rarest manuscripts in the world—a gold-leaf copy of Shahnameh."

"What's Shahnameh?" Tasha asked, manoeuvring around a car that had inexplicably decided to cruise at 30 km/h in the fast lane.

"It's an 11th-century Persian epic poem," Indro explained. "Full of myths, legends, and the kind of drama that makes Bollywood look subtle."

"Sounds fancy," Tasha said. "Do they let you read it, or is it just for show?"

"They let you read it," Indro said, "if you can convince the librarian that you're not a threat to its existence."

"Good luck with that," Tasha muttered. "I once got side-eyed for asking for a ballpoint pen at the Sassoon Library."

They approached the end of the bridge, where the toll booths had given way to sprawling lanes that filtered cars into Bandra's chaos. The transition was almost poetic—smooth, serene order dissolving into the frenzied rhythm of city life.

"You know," Tasha said, her voice softer now, "I like libraries. They're like little time capsules. You walk in, and suddenly you're not in the present anymore."

Indro glanced at her, surprised by the shift in tone. "That's... a surprisingly tender thing to say."

"Don't get used to it," she shot back, her grin returning. "I'm still the ruthless toll booth queen."

He laughed, but the warmth of her comment lingered, weaving itself into the rhythm of their journey as they merged into the next stretch of road.

The SUV glided off the Sea Link with the kind of confidence that only a car driven by Tasha could manage—a mix of steely determination and sheer audacity. The sign loomed ahead, vague as a politician's promise:

"Bandra Reclamation ↗ | Continue to Western Express Highway ↔"

"What does this even mean?" Tasha asked, her tone bordering on incredulity. "Do we ascend to Reclamation heaven or continue to purgatory?"

"It's a metaphor," Indro said, his finger tapping his temple in mock wisdom. "Mumbai is teaching us to embrace uncertainty."

"Uncertainty is fine," Tasha snapped. "Getting lost is not."

She chose what seemed like the logical path—except that logic in Mumbai roads is as rare as an on-time suburban train. A few seconds later, they were funnelling down a narrow, dusty stretch with no apparent destination in sight.

"This doesn't feel like Reclamation," Indro observed, peering at the construction debris littering the roadside.

"Unless they're reclaiming their ability to confuse people," Tasha muttered, jerking the wheel to avoid a stray dog and a cart piled high with crates that seemed moments away from toppling.

The SUV finally reached a landmark: a massive Bollywood billboard featuring an actor mid-leap, arms spread wide as though auditioning for a deodorant ad. Under its ostentatious shadow stood Kabir and Aria, the mismatched duo looking distinctly unimpressed with their situation. Kabir waved with the enthusiasm of someone flagging down rescue, while Aria, ever poised, sipped from a water bottle and adjusted her sunhat with queenly disdain.

Tasha rolled down the window. "This your new hangout spot? Waiting for autographs?"

Kabir grinned. "We're waiting for deliverance. Does your chariot come with AC?"

"And snacks," Aria added as she climbed into the backseat. "I'm starving."

"Snacks?" Indro asked, twisting in his seat. "You didn't bring any for us?"

"We're the guests!" Kabir declared, settling in. "Guests don't bring snacks."

"Guests don't demand them either," Tasha quipped, jockeying the car back onto the main road—or what she hoped was the main road.

The ride resumed, albeit with a slight air of chaos, as Tasha navigated toward the next decision point. A sign came into view, more bewildering than helpful:

"BKC ↔ | Dharavi ↗ | Sion ↖"

"Great," Tasha muttered. "Three choices, no idea. It's like Mumbai's version of a reality show."

"Pick Dharavi!" Kabir piped up, leaning forward excitedly. "We can get kababs and Bluetooth speakers."

Aria rolled her eyes. "We're not stopping for your shopping spree."

"Or kababs," Indro added. "We're already late."

Tasha sighed and took the left turn, leading them toward the maze-like expanse of Kalanagar Junction. It was a symphony of honks, screeches, and indecipherable hand gestures as vehicles tried to outmanoeuvre one another with the finesse of warring chess pieces.

"What is this place?" Aria asked, clutching her sunhat. "A driving academy for chaos?"

"It's the heart of Mumbai," Indro said solemnly. "And the heart always skips a few beats."

They were soon crawling through traffic at a speed that could be measured in inches per minute. Tasha's patience, however, moved at a much faster pace—toward its limit.

To lighten the mood, Indro turned to Kabir and Aria. "So, is it true you two met fighting over a book?"

Kabir groaned. "Can we not talk about that?"

"Oh, we absolutely can," Aria said with relish. "It was at Shemaroo Library in Kemps Corner. We both wanted the same copy of Baldacci's Long Shadows. I got there first, of course."

Kabir leaned forward, mock-serious. "Barely. She swooped in like a hawk."

"Because I'm faster," Aria said sweetly, "and smarter."

"And meaner," Kabir muttered. "Do you know what she did? She spoiled the ending."

Aria smirked. "Not my fault you didn't read fast enough."

"Not fast enough?" Kabir exploded. "You told me who the murderer was before I could even check out the book!"

Aria leaned back, smug. "It's a Baldacci novel. The thrill isn't in who did it; it's in how."

Indro laughed. "She's got a point. Also, this is the most romantic library story I've ever heard."

"Romantic?" Kabir said, scandalized. "It was war."

"And yet, here you are," Tasha said, smirking through the rearview mirror. "Bickering like an old married couple."

Aria reached over to pat Kabir's shoulder. "Admit it—you love me for my literary ruthlessness."

Kabir groaned but didn't argue.

After what felt like an eternity, the SUV finally cleared the maze of Kalanagar Junction. Tasha accelerated with the enthusiasm of someone escaping prison, her knuckles relaxing on the wheel for the first time in an hour.

"Well," she said, glancing at the group, "if that wasn't the scenic route, I don't know what is."

Kabir leaned forward again. "So, what's next? Snacks? Music? Another detour?"

Tasha grinned. "Stick around. This ride's got plenty more twists."

The SUV roared ahead, and for a moment, the chaos of Mumbai faded into laughter and camaraderie, their journey as unpredictable—and entertaining—as the city itself.

The SUV rolled through Bandra's chaotic streets, past stretches of uneven pavement and spontaneous roadblocks courtesy of rogue vendors and opportunistic pigeons. Tasha was steering with her usual precision, navigating the mayhem as if it were a video game where only she knew the cheat codes.

"Slow down!" Aria suddenly exclaimed, pointing out the window. "Look there, by the rubble."

Tasha braked expertly, her SUV gliding to a dignified stop at the curb. "If this is another mysterious civic wonder, I'm not impressed."

"It's a cat," Aria clarified, already unbuckling her seatbelt. "And we're taking it."

Perched atop a pile of construction debris was a regal orange cat, its green eyes scanning the scene with detached authority. It looked as though it had been waiting for an entourage.

"Let me guess," Indro said. "Another Nugget?"

"Every cat is a Nugget," Tasha replied, stepping out to join Aria. "Golden treasures in a sea of human incompetence."

Kabir groaned from the backseat. "This is how it starts. First, it's 'just a cat.' Next thing you know, we're stopping for every stray in Mumbai."

Aria crouched near the cat, extending a hand. "Come here, Nugget. You've been promoted to backseat royalty."

The cat stared for a moment, then sauntered over as if granting an audience. Without hesitation, it leapt into the SUV and curled up on Kabir's lap.

"Why me?" Kabir protested, holding his hands aloft. "I didn't sign up for this."

"You didn't sign up for clean signage or proper lanes either," Tasha said as she slid back into the driver's seat. "But here we are."

With Nugget now firmly ensconced, the SUV resumed its journey, navigating Bandra's narrow streets with the precision of a surgeon and the nerves of a gambler. The conversation naturally veered toward the state of civic sense—or the lack thereof.

"Why is it," Tasha began, manoeuvring around a scooter that had parked itself in the middle of the road, "that this city can build world-class flyovers but can't teach people how to use a roundabout?"

"Because infrastructure's easy," Indro replied. "Behaviour change is hard."

"Exactly," Aria chimed in. "You can build all the Coastal Roads and Sea Links you want, but if people don't follow basic rules, what's the point?"

Kabir, still trying to adjust Nugget's weight on his lap, sighed. "And don't get me started on signage. Half the roads don't have any signs. The other half have signs so vague they might as well be riddles."

"It's not just roads," Aria added. "Libraries face the same problem. They're supposed to be public resources, but they're so underfunded and inaccessible that most people don't even know they exist."

They passed the MCubed Library on D'Monte Park Road, its modest façade lit softly by the golden light of sunset.

"Take this place," Indro said, gesturing toward the building. "It's a shining example of what libraries should be— community-driven, inclusive, and actively engaging with the neighborhood."

"Remember that time they hosted a lit fest?" Aria asked. "Half the people came for the poetry, the other half for the samosas."

"And everyone left happy," Kabir added. "Now that's what I call civic success."

Tasha smiled. "Libraries should be like that—welcoming and useful, not just monuments to what we used to care about."

As they approached another intersection, the SUV slowed behind a car that had decided to stop abruptly, its driver honking furiously at nothing.

"Here we go," Tasha muttered. "The Great Mumbai Honk-a-thon."

Kabir rolled down the window. "What's he honking at? The light's red."

"He's honking at life," Indro replied. "It's a form of catharsis."

"Or confusion," Aria said. "Maybe he thinks if he honks hard enough, the light will change."

As the light turned green and the SUV surged forward, the conversation circled back to civic sense—or its absence.

"Honestly," Tasha said, "if people in this city showed half as much care for public spaces as they do for honking, Mumbai would be a paradise."

Aria nodded. "It's not just about following rules; it's about respecting shared spaces. Roads, libraries—they're all part of the same ecosystem."

"Exactly," Indro agreed. "It's like Nugget here. He respects the SUV. Doesn't claw the seats, doesn't steal snacks."

Kabir glanced at the cat sprawled contentedly across his lap. "Speak for yourself. He's been eyeing my sandwich since we left Bandra."

As the SUV glided back toward South Bombay, the sunset bathed the skyline in warm hues, and the chaos of the day began to mellow into something almost poetic. Nugget, now dozing, occasionally flicked his tail in response to the group's chatter.

"You know," Indro said, staring out the window, "for all its flaws, this city has its moments."

"It does," Tasha agreed, steering into the smooth curve of Marine Drive. "But it wouldn't hurt if those moments came with better signage and fewer potholes."

"And more libraries," Aria added. "With parking. And maybe a café."

Kabir smirked. "And valet cats. Nugget could lead the way."

The group laughed, the kind of easy, unfiltered laughter that only comes when friends share the absurdities of life. As they pulled into their final stop, Tasha turned off the engine and glanced at the rearview mirror.

"Well, team," she said, her voice warm. "We made it. Chaos and all."

Aria smiled. "Not just chaos. Companionship. And a little perspective."

Kabir looked down at Nugget, who was now curled into a perfect circle. "And a cat. Don't forget the cat."

With that, the group stepped out into the cool evening air, their journey—equal parts ridiculous and revelatory—now another story to tell. Nugget leapt onto Tasha's shoulder, his tail flicking with the confidence of someone who knew exactly where he belonged. And as the group walked off together, the streets of Mumbai—chaotic, unpredictable, and full of stories—seemed ready for their next adventure.

Chapter 10

Mastery in Sickness, Mastery in Health

The taxi meandered through Parel's bustling streets, its horn contributing to the city's symphony of sounds. Tasha and Indro sat in the backseat, observing the vibrant tapestry of life unfolding outside.

As they approached King Edward Memorial (KEM) Hospital, the sidewalks transformed into a lively marketplace. Vendors displayed an array of goods—fresh fruits, colorful bangles, and an assortment of street foods—each stall a testament to Mumbai's entrepreneurial spirit.

"It's fascinating," Indro remarked, "how necessity breeds such vibrant street commerce."

Tasha nodded. "Indeed. Though, I wonder how the hospital manages with all this activity at its doorstep."

The taxi slowed near the hospital entrance, where a sign declared, "No Hawking Zone." Despite the notice, vendors continued their trade unabated.

"It seems the sign is more of a suggestion," Indro observed with a wry smile.

Tasha chuckled. "In Mumbai, signs often serve as mere decoration."

The driver pulled over, and as they settled the fare, Tasha glanced around. "I hope finding a parking spot here isn't as challenging as navigating through the city."

Indro raised an eyebrow. "Considering Mumbai's vehicular population has surpassed 48 lakh, with over 14 lakh private cars, I'd say parking is a luxury."

Tasha sighed. "I read that the Brihanmumbai Municipal Corporation is planning to develop new parking spots to accommodate over 22,000 vehicles across four densely populated wards. But I suppose that's a drop in the ocean."

They stepped out of the taxi, immediately enveloped by the city's humid embrace. Navigating through the throng of people, they approached the hospital's entrance. The grand facade of KEM Hospital stood as a beacon of hope amidst the urban sprawl.

"Did you know," Indro began, "KEM Hospital treats about 1.8 million outpatients and 85,000 inpatients annually? It's one of Mumbai's largest healthcare institutions."

Tasha looked up at the building, her expression softening. "It's remarkable how it continues to serve so many, despite the challenges."

As they entered the hospital, the cacophony of the streets faded, replaced by the subdued hum typical of medical facilities. Tasha glanced back once more at the vibrant scene outside before the doors closed behind them.

"Let's hope our visit here is as smooth as our journey," she murmured, stepping into the hospital's quieter realm.

Inside the hospital, the corridors hummed with the quiet urgency of a place that never truly rested. Patients sat on benches, clutching prescription slips like lifelines, while families gathered in small clusters, their voices lowered but charged with concern. The faint smell of antiseptic lingered in the air, mingling with the aroma of samosas someone had sneaked in from a nearby hawker stall.

Tasha and Indro wove their way through the labyrinth of activity, finally spotting a familiar figure reclining on a hospital bed near the far end of the ward. Datta, the elderly security guard from Tasha's childhood building, looked up just as they approached. His face, lined with years of experience and a stubborn resilience, broke into a wide smile.

"Tasha beti!" he exclaimed, attempting to sit up straighter. "And who's this?" He gestured toward Indro with a curious glance.

"This is Indro," Tasha said, her tone warm. "He's… part of the entourage today."

Indro extended a hand. "Pleased to meet you, Datta. I've heard a lot about you."

"Good things, I hope," Datta replied, his handshake firm despite his evident fatigue. "Though Tasha probably exaggerated. She always had a knack for turning small stories into epics."

"Still does," Indro quipped, earning a mock glare from Tasha.

They pulled up two chairs and settled in. Tasha immediately noticed the bandages peeking out from under Datta's hospital gown. "What happened?" she asked, concern lacing her voice.

"Nothing serious," Datta replied, waving her off. "A small surgery. Just a part of growing old, I suppose. They patched me up well enough here, but the waiting was something else. You'd think the hospital was running a city-wide festival with the number of people here."

Datta gestured toward the crowded ward. "You see this? They're doing their best, but it's like trying to empty the sea with a bucket. Patients coming in from all over the state, sometimes the country, and not enough staff or beds to go around."

"Must be overwhelming," Indro said, glancing around. "How do they manage?"

"They don't always," Datta admitted. "But I'll tell you this—these doctors and nurses are warriors. They work miracles with what little they have. The problem isn't them; it's the system. And sometimes, us."

"Us?" Tasha asked, leaning forward.

Datta nodded. "Patients and families treating this place like a public park. Littering in the corridors, crowding waiting areas. I saw someone eating peanuts and tossing the shells right under their chair yesterday."

Indro frowned. "In a hospital?"

"Exactly," Datta said. "If everyone just respected the space, it'd make things a lot easier. But we take these places for granted until we're the ones in the beds."

Tasha changed the subject slightly, sensing the need for levity. "What about the hawkers outside? I saw someone selling umbrellas and cucumbers at the gate."

Datta chuckled. "Those hawkers are the unofficial staff of this hospital. Need tea? A quick snack? A pair of socks? They've got you covered. And they don't take breaks."

"They must be helpful for people who can't afford the hospital canteen," Indro noted.

"Helpful, yes," Datta agreed, "but also a menace. Yesterday, an ambulance couldn't get through because a chaiwallah had parked his cart too close to the gate. The driver nearly had a heart attack himself, honking and shouting."

"Did they move?" Tasha asked.

"Eventually," Datta said with a grin. "But not before selling two cups of tea to the ambulance driver."

Indro laughed. "Talk about customer service."

Datta's expression turned thoughtful. "You know, it's easy to blame them, but these hawkers are just trying to survive. It's the lack of proper planning that creates this mess. If the city gave them designated spaces, it'd be better for everyone."

Tasha nodded. "That's true. But it's also about personal responsibility. People could help by keeping the hospital clean, using the bins, and not crowding the corridors."

"Exactly," Datta said. "Small things, but they make a big difference. And let's not forget the importance of patience. Everyone's in a rush to be seen first, but if they just waited their turn, things would run a lot smoother."

The conversation drifted to lighter topics—memories of Tasha's childhood, Datta chasing after mischievous kids in the building, and the time he'd convinced a delivery boy to carry groceries up five flights of stairs because the elevator was out of order.

"Those were simpler times," Datta said with a nostalgic smile.

Tasha patted his hand. "And you're still the same, Datta. Tough as nails and full of stories."

"I try," he said. "Now go on, both of you. Don't waste your day sitting here with an old man."

As they rose to leave, Tasha hesitated. "Do you need anything? Should we bring you something?"

Datta shook his head. "Just come back soon. Visits like this are better medicine than anything they give me here."

Indro smiled. "You're in good hands, Datta. And with your resilience, you'll be out of here before the chaiwala runs out of tea."

With a laugh and a wave, they left the ward, stepping back into the hospital's bustling corridors, their minds brimming with reflections on the resilience and quirks of the city's heart.

Leaving the ward, Tasha and Indro navigated the bustling hospital corridors, their conversation naturally drifting to the scenes they'd encountered outside. The vendors at the hospital gate were still firmly etched in Tasha's mind—cucumbers stacked like green sentinels, chai brewing with the urgency of a military operation, and an odd assortment of plastic sandals and phone chargers vying for attention.

"I'm curious," Tasha began, glancing at Indro. "How is it that hawkers can set up shop outside a hospital entrance without anyone batting an eyelid?"

"It's not that simple," Indro replied. "There's a whole law for this—the Street Vendors Act of 2014. It's supposed to regulate hawking while protecting livelihoods. But implementing it? That's another story."

Indro gestured toward the hospital gates as they passed. "See that? Hawkers encroach on sidewalks and entrances, leaving no room for wheelchairs, stretchers, or even regular pedestrians. Imagine trying to navigate that with a broken leg."

"It's not just patients," Tasha added. "What about ambulances? One chai cart in the wrong spot could cost someone their life."

"And then there's the hygiene issue," Indro continued. "Hawkers lack access to proper sanitation facilities. Combine that with the crowds they attract, and it's a perfect storm for spreading infections—right outside a healthcare facility, no less."

"Especially in a hospital," Tasha said, her voice tinged with frustration. "Isn't there some irony in risking an infection while trying to recover from one?"

Tasha sighed, watching a hawker expertly balance a tray of vada pav while shouting out offers. "And I suppose trying to regulate this is like catching water in a sieve."

Indro nodded. "Exactly. Most hawking is informal, so tracking or monitoring is nearly impossible. Uncollected waste piles up. Food safety? Let's just say your samosa might come with a side of unwashed hands."

"What if we had dedicated hawking zones around hospitals?" Tasha suggested. "Somewhere close enough to be convenient but far enough to avoid blocking access."

"That's part of the law," Indro said. "The challenge is enforcement. But hawkers could also self-regulate. Form associations, set boundaries, and keep their areas clean."

"And maybe," Tasha mused, "add shared dustbins that hawkers are responsible for. It's not just their customers littering—it's their business at stake."

"Exactly," Indro said. "A little accountability goes a long way. Plus, the hospital could collaborate with local authorities to set up sanitation points nearby."

Indro paused as they reached a shaded corridor. "You know what's missing? Communication. Put up clear, multilingual signs about hawking rules and hygiene. Maybe even a few workshops for hawkers on food safety."

Tasha raised an eyebrow. "Workshops? That's optimistic. But it's not a bad idea. Education's half the battle."

As they exited the hospital building, their conversation briefly paused. A young boy zipped past, balancing a tray of steaming tea cups like a circus act. Behind him, a woman argued with a customer over the price of cucumbers, her baby snoozing on a makeshift cradle of vegetable sacks.

Tasha couldn't help but smile. "You have to admit, there's something admirable about their hustle."

Indro chuckled. "Admirable? Yes. Practical? Not always. But in a city like this, survival comes first."

She nodded thoughtfully. "Maybe that's the real problem. Everyone's just trying to survive, and the bigger picture gets lost."

As they reached the gate, Tasha spotted a discarded surgical mask lying near a bin, the wind teasing it along the pavement. She picked it up, tossing it into the trash.

Indro raised an eyebrow. "Civic sense in action?"

"Leading by example," she replied with a grin. "Now let's see if the rest of the city follows."

The hospital cafeteria was a curious mix of functionality and chaos—long metal tables lined with an odd assortment of mismatched chairs, walls painted a shade of beige that might once have been cheerful, and the faint aroma of samosas battling valiantly against the more industrial scent of over-boiled tea. Tasha and Indro found a spot near the corner, next to a man furiously scribbling on a notepad and a woman cradling a bowl of dal like it was her last lifeline.

"This," Indro declared, settling into his chair, "is the nerve centre of the hospital. Forget the operating theatres or the labs—true humanity is dissected here."

Tasha raised an eyebrow. "I didn't realize cafeteria dal could inspire philosophical musings."

Indro placed his stainless-steel protein shaker on the table with a flourish. "It's not the dal, Tasha. It's about observing life's rhythm." He unscrewed the lid confidently, ready to sip his signature homemade protein shake. But as he tilted the bottle, a series of unfortunate events unfolded in cinematic slow motion.

The lid, improperly tightened in a rare lapse of Indro's perfectionism, gave way with a dramatic pop. A fountain of viscous, beige liquid erupted, coating his face, shirt, and even the elderly gentleman at the adjacent table.

"Great Scott!" Indro gasped, as Tasha froze, torn between horror and hilarity. The elderly man wiped his glasses with a napkin, giving Indro a bemused look. "Is this your idea of modern art, young man?"

"I… I can explain," Indro stammered, grabbing handfuls of tissues from the dispenser. Tasha, struggling to contain her laughter, handed him her handkerchief.

"You're right, Indro," she said, eyes sparkling with mirth. "This is the nerve center of the hospital. And you just gave everyone a dose of nerve tonic."

The room, initially silent in shock, burst into laughter. Even the cafeteria staff chuckled as they brought a mop and bucket to clean the floor.

"Let this be a lesson," Indro muttered, dabbing at his shirt. "Always tighten your protein shaker lid. And never underestimate dal as a safer meal option."

Tasha grinned. "Or the audience in a hospital cafeteria. You've just made their day."

To bring balance to the moment, a heated argument erupted at the counter. A man in a crumpled shirt was berating the cashier over the price of a plate of idli.

"Forty rupees for two idlis?" he demanded, his voice rising. "Are these made of gold?"

The cashier, unperturbed, replied, "If you want affordable, there's a man outside selling vada pav for fifteen."

"Exactly!" the man snapped. "But my doctor said no fried food. So now I'm stuck paying forty!"

Tasha turned to Indro. "See? It's not just philosophy. It's economics."

As they sipped their tea—too sweet for Tasha's liking and too weak for Indro's—they overheard snippets of conversations from the neighboring tables.

One man, with his leg in a cast, complained about the difficulty of navigating the hospital's crowded hallways. "It's like an obstacle course," he said, grimacing. "Wheelchairs, stretchers, hawkers selling tea—all in a single file."

"Don't forget the family reunions in the waiting area," added a woman. "I had to step over three suitcases and an entire picnic setup to get to my appointment."

Another patient chimed in, gesturing animatedly with a spoon. "It's not just the crowds. The litter! I saw a guy toss a water bottle right under the 'Keep Clean' sign."

"Classic," Tasha whispered to Indro. "Do you think people see those signs as challenges?"

Indro smiled. "Probably. Like, 'I dare you to ignore this.'"

As they finished their tea, a young doctor in a white coat plopped into the chair opposite them, looking like he'd just run a marathon in a war zone.

"Mind if I sit here?" he asked, already lowering himself. "It's the only seat not directly under the fan. I'd rather sweat than catch pneumonia."

"Please," Tasha said, gesturing to the seat. "You look like you've earned it."

He sighed deeply, rubbing his temples. "I swear, if one more patient shows me a WhatsApp forward about garlic curing diabetes, I'm going to prescribe them a crash course in critical thinking."

Indro chuckled. "Rough day?"

"Rough week," the doctor replied. "And it's only Tuesday."

The doctor leaned back in his chair, cradling his tea like a lifeline. "You know what the problem is? It's not the patients—it's the everything else. The noise, the hawkers, the families who think the hospital is a five-star hotel."

Tasha tilted her head. "Five-star hotel?"

"Oh yes," he said, nodding vigorously. "They want extra pillows, AC that works, and chai delivered to their bedside. Meanwhile, I'm running between wards trying to convince people that Google is not a substitute for a medical degree."

Indro smiled. "And the hawkers?"

"They're a blessing and a curse," the doctor admitted. "Where else can you get chai at two in the morning? But when their carts block the ambulance bay, I lose my temper. Once, I saw a chaiwallah sell tea to the ambulance driver before moving his cart. The sheer audacity!"

Tasha, always one for practicality, asked, "So what's the solution? Ban hawkers completely?"

"Not entirely," the doctor said. "They're part of the ecosystem. But there needs to be regulation—designated vending zones, maybe a bit farther from the entrance. And the hospital could use more trash bins. You'd be surprised how much litter comes from families camping out for days."

Indro added, "And maybe a few workshops for patients on hospital etiquette. Like, don't argue with the doctor about WhatsApp cures."

The doctor smiled faintly. "If you can get people to attend, you'd deserve a Nobel."

As they rose to leave, the doctor waved them off. "Enjoy the rest of your day. And if you see a hawker selling garlic as a miracle cure, send him my way. I'll have a word."

Tasha grinned. "Consider it done."

As they stepped out of the cafeteria, Indro turned to her. "You know, this might be the most enlightening lunch I've ever had."

"Enlightening, yes," Tasha said. "But I wouldn't recommend the tea."

Leaving the cafeteria, Tasha and Indro walked toward the hospital's side gate, the late afternoon sun casting long shadows on the uneven pavement. The gate was a quieter spot compared to the bustling main entrance, but it wasn't without its own activity. A small cluster of vendors had set up shop near a banyan tree, their colorful wares spread out on worn mats. Among them was a young girl, no older than ten, threading delicate white mogra flowers into garlands with nimble fingers.

Tasha stopped in her tracks, the scent of the blossoms tugging at something deep and familiar in her memory. "Wait a second," she said, pulling Indro toward the girl. "Mogra. I can't resist."

The girl looked up with bright eyes and a gap-toothed grin. "Fresh mogra, didi. Five rupees a string."

"You had me at mogra," Tasha said, crouching to take a closer look. "How many can I buy without bankrupting you?"

"All of them if you want," the girl said cheekily, holding up her handiwork. "But leave some for the others, or my mother will scold me."

Indro leaned against the tree, observing the scene. "And here I thought mogra negotiations weren't a thing."

"They are now," Tasha said, smiling as she handed over a ten-rupee note. "Two, please."

As the girl carefully wrapped the garlands in a leaf, Tasha struck up a conversation. "What's your name?"

"Radha," the girl replied, her fingers never stopping. "I help my mother sell flowers after school."

"Do you like it?" Tasha asked.

Radha shrugged. "It's okay. I like school more, but this helps us buy books and pay fees."

Indro, always the pragmatist, chimed in. "Do you ever get into trouble selling near the hospital?"

Radha giggled. "Only when the watchman sees us. Then we run. But he's old, so we don't have to run far."

Tasha laughed, impressed by the girl's frankness. "That's some strategy."

As Radha finished her work, Tasha turned thoughtful. "You know, it's funny how hawkers and vendors like Radha are such a vital part of the city, but they're always on the edge of being chased away."

Indro nodded. "It's the eternal balancing act. They provide convenience, but at the cost of order. And it's not their fault—it's the lack of proper spaces for them to work."

Tasha looked back at Radha, now threading more flowers. "It's a shame. She's smart, resourceful. But instead of just chasing her away, the system could support her. Designated vending spots, basic facilities—it's not rocket science."

"And maybe a little compassion," Indro added. "It wouldn't hurt to think of them as people trying to survive rather than just obstacles in the way."

As Tasha and Indro prepared to leave, garlands in hand, a loud crash erupted near a cart selling tender coconuts. Heads turned as the vendor scrambled to pick up a coconut that had rolled into the middle of the pathway and lodged itself firmly under the wheel of a hospital stretcher.

A young man pushing the stretcher—clearly not prepared for coconut-related emergencies—stopped mid-stride, staring at the rogue fruit as if it were a ticking time bomb. The patient on the stretcher, a bespectacled elderly gentleman, craned his neck to see what the holdup was.

"Beta, is this the part where I get hit with the coconut?" he asked, deadpan, earning muffled laughter from the growing crowd.

The vendor, undeterred, darted forward, deftly grabbing the coconut and flashing a toothy grin. "No charge for this one!" he announced triumphantly, holding it aloft like a trophy.

Tasha couldn't help but laugh. "Now that's customer service."

The young man, still wide-eyed, maneuvered the stretcher around the vendor's cart, muttering something about needing hazard pay. The elderly patient, however, seemed thoroughly amused.

"You don't see this in the private hospitals," he declared, settling back onto the stretcher. "All they have there are boring air-conditioned corridors. No adventure."

As the scene dispersed, Tasha turned to Indro, shaking her head. "You can't script moments like that. Only here would a coconut cause traffic."

"And yet, everyone keeps moving," Indro replied. "That's the beauty of it. The chaos, the resilience—it all works somehow."

Tasha smiled, slipping the mogra garlands into her bag. "Maybe we could all learn a thing or two from that coconut vendor. Adapt, improvise, keep going."

"And throw in some humour while you're at it," Indro added. "It makes the bumps—literal and metaphorical—a little easier."

With that, they walked toward the hospital gates, the scent of mogra mingling with the din of voices and the distant hum of the city beyond.

As Tasha and Indro approached the hospital gates, a sudden commotion drew their attention. An ambulance screeched to a halt, and paramedics emerged, carefully wheeling out a woman whose body bore the unmistakable signs of severe burns. The gravity of her condition was palpable, casting a somber shadow over the scene.

Tasha's expression softened with concern. "Indro, seeing her reminds me of the critical need for skin donations in our country. Burn victims often suffer immensely due to the scarcity of available skin grafts."

Indro nodded, his tone reflecting the seriousness of the topic. "You're right, Tasha. Skin donation is a post-mortem procedure that can significantly aid burn patients. Unfortunately, a lack of awareness and prevalent superstitions hinder its widespread adoption."

Tasha tilted her head, curiosity piqued. "Superstitions? Like what?"

Indro sighed. "Many people believe that donating skin will lead to disfigurement in the afterlife or affect their next birth. These myths, deeply rooted in cultural beliefs, deter families from consenting to skin donation."

Tasha frowned. "That's disheartening. Especially when the process is straightforward and can save lives."

Indro continued, "In India, the Transplantation of Human Organs Act governs organ and tissue donations. Skin can be harvested within six hours of death, from areas like the back and thighs, without causing visible disfigurement. Facilities like the National Burns Centre in Mumbai have been pivotal in promoting skin donation, but the demand still far exceeds the supply."

Tasha's eyes reflected a mix of sadness and determination. "It seems like a combination of education and empathy is needed to change these perceptions."

Indro agreed. "Absolutely. Public awareness campaigns and community engagement can help dispel these myths.

Encouraging conversations about the importance and impact of skin donation is crucial."

As they pondered this, a commotion nearby caught their attention. A young intern, balancing a tray of medical supplies, stumbled as he dodged a loose football kicked by a child outside the waiting area. The ball skidded into the legs of an unsuspecting passerby, who laughed good-naturedly and returned it to the boy.

Tasha smiled softly. "For the sake of those who suffer, like the woman we just saw, it's the least we can do—to advocate, educate, and bring some light into such dark moments."

Indro gave a nod, his gaze steady. "Even in moments like these, small acts can make a world of difference."

They continued toward the gates, a shared understanding deepening between them, the earlier levity giving way to a quiet resolve about the roles they could play in fostering change.

As Tasha and Indro hailed a taxi, a cycle rickshaw zipped by, its cargo of steel rods swaying precariously. The driver pulled up, his cab sporting an air freshener shaped like a Christmas tree that smelled faintly of petrol and lemons.

They clambered in, Tasha pulling the door shut with the care of someone who had once dealt with a loose hinge. The cab inched forward, joining the slow-moving cavalcade of cars, rickshaws, and the occasional bullock cart.

"You know," Indro began, watching a pedestrian casually jaywalk through traffic, "there's something remarkable about how people navigate spaces here. It's a miracle no one's constantly colliding."

"That's because there are rules," Tasha quipped. "Unwritten ones. Like, don't trust a zebra crossing and always assume the guy next to you has no brakes."

As they waited for the car to merge into the thick flow of vehicles, Tasha sighed. "Do you suppose we should offer extra for a driver who promises not to narrate his life story?"

Indro chuckled. "I'd pay double if he promises not to play Bollywood remixes from the early 2000s."

The driver, blissfully unaware of their preferences, flicked on the radio. A nostalgic jingle crackled through the static, promising a medley of evergreen hits. Tasha raised an eyebrow. "If this is from a playlist labelled 'Evergreen,' I'm walking."

Tasha pointed out a stretch of road devoid of proper pedestrian crossings. "Look at that. People are weaving through cars like they're auditioning for an action movie. Why is it so hard to paint a few lines?" As they passed a footpath overtaken by hawkers, Indro sighed. "If we could reclaim even half the sidewalks, the roads wouldn't look like this." The taxi slowed near a bus stop overflowing with commuters. "And then there's this," Tasha added, gesturing at the crowd. "Every bus is packed like a can of sardines. No wonder people prefer their own cars."

"People could at least cross at corners," Indro said. "It wouldn't solve everything, but it'd reduce the risk of drivers treating pedestrians like slalom poles." "And hawkers," Tasha added, "need proper vending zones. This constant battle for footpaths is exhausting—for them and us." Indro nodded. "Imagine if we had reliable buses and trains. The roads wouldn't look like the set of a disaster movie."

As the taxi reached a narrow stretch of road, a small orange cat ambled across, pausing in the middle with the confidence of a traffic officer. The cab screeched to a halt, the driver muttering something inaudible.

"That's Nugget," Indro said without hesitation, leaning forward. "Clearly."

Tasha blinked, turning toward him. "Did you just… name the cat?"

"Of course," Indro replied. "What else would you call it?"

Tasha was quiet for a moment, a smile tugging at her lips. The simplicity of the gesture—a name, shared without preamble—was unexpectedly touching. "Welcome to the Nugget Club," she said softly. "Membership comes with infinite patience and the ability to spot a good story in any feline."

The cab waited as Nugget eventually moved on, tail flicking in triumph. Tasha used the pause to glance around. "Look at that," she said, gesturing at the street vendors neatly aligned along the curb. "They've actually organized themselves."

"It's impressive," Indro agreed. "Proof that self-regulation works when there's mutual respect." They discussed how hawkers could work with local authorities to create orderly, accessible vending areas. "Imagine if this was standard," Tasha said. "No more blocked footpaths, no more fights with pedestrians." They passed a trash-strewn corner. "And if we had enough bins," Indro added, "maybe people would stop tossing garbage wherever they pleased."

The driver restarted the cab, glancing in the rearview mirror. "That cat's smarter than half the people on the road," he muttered, breaking the mood with perfect timing.

Tasha laughed. "He's got a point. Nugget didn't need a license or a GPS to take control of that intersection."

"And he left the place cleaner than most humans," Indro added, earning another grin from Tasha.

The ride continued, the conversation flowing as easily as the city's unstoppable rhythm. By the time they reached their destination, the warmth of shared ideas and lighthearted banter had filled the cab like an invisible passenger.

As they stepped out, Tasha turned to Indro, her tone teasing but warm. "You know, calling the cat Nugget was surprisingly thoughtful."

"Thoughtful?" Indro replied, raising an eyebrow. "I just thought it suited the little tyrant."

She smiled, shaking her head. "Still. It means you're starting to get it—naming the cats, embracing the detours. That's life, really. Messy, unpredictable, but infinitely interesting."

Indro held the door for her as they walked toward the café. "And all the better when shared," he said lightly.

The city seemed to hum in agreement, its stories continuing as their own chapter drew to a close.

THE END